SPRINKLES AND SWIRLS

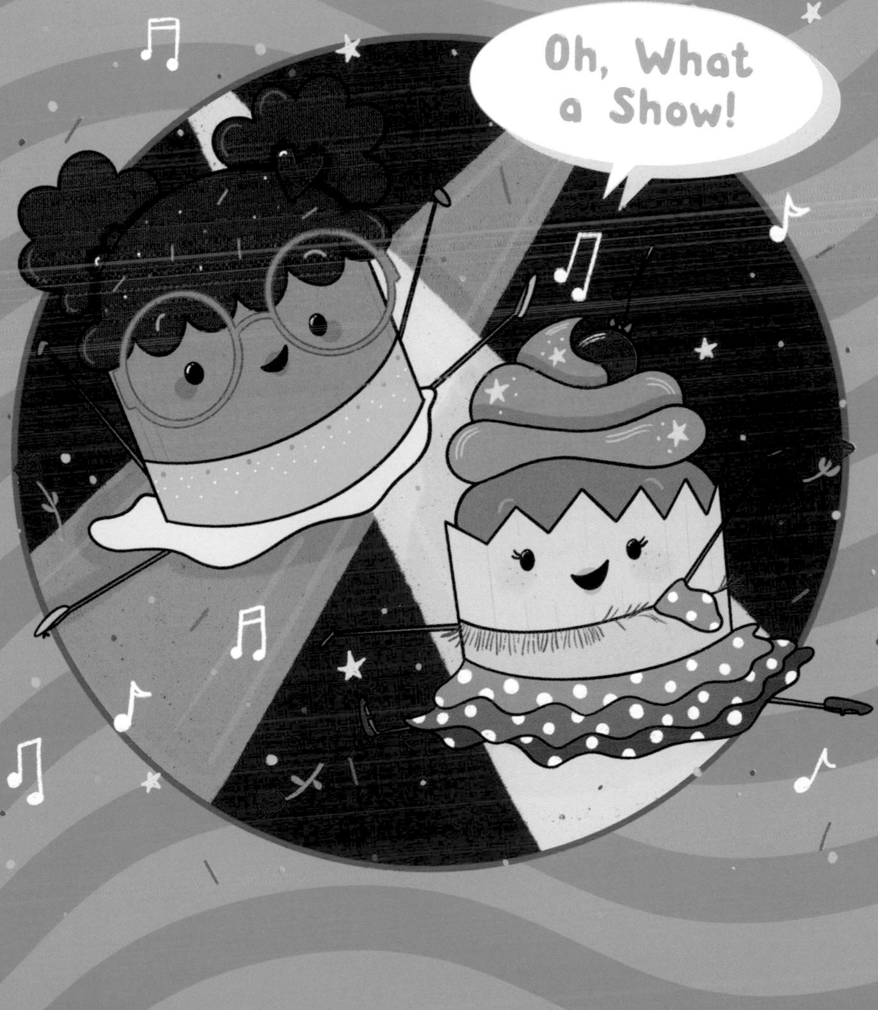
Oh, What a Show!

For sweet Octavia —L. S.

Dedicated to Emilia and Anina who are always ready for a good talent show! —S. A.

SIMON SPOTLIGHT
An imprint of Simon & Schuster Children's Publishing Division
1230 Avenue of the Americas, New York, New York 10020
This Simon Spotlight edition September 2022
Text copyright © 2022 by Lola M. Schaefer
Illustrations copyright © 2022 by Savannah Allen
For information about special discounts for bulk purchases, please contact Simon & Schuster Special
Sales at 1-866-506-1949 or business@simonandschuster.com.
Manufactured in China 0522 SCP
2 4 6 8 10 9 7 5 3 1
Library of Congress Cataloging-in-Publication Data
Names: Schaefer, Lola M., 1950- author. | Allen, Savannah, illustrator. Title: Oh, what a show! /
by Lola M. Schaefer ; illustrated by Savannah Allen. Description: Simon Spotlight edition. |
New York : Simon Spotlight, 2022. | Series: Sprinkles and Swirls | Audience: Ages 4-6. | Audience:
Grades K-1. | Summary: Cupcakes Sprinkles and Swirls decide to perform in the talent show, but first
need to decide what talent they want to showcase. Identifiers: LCCN 2021053464 (print) |
LCCN 2021053465 (ebook) | ISBN 9781665917957 (hardcover) | ISBN 9781665917964 (paperback) |
ISBN 9781665917971 (ebook) Subjects: CYAC: Graphic novels. | Cupcakes—Fiction. |
Talent shows—Fiction. | LCGFT: Graphic novels. Classification: LCC PZ7.7.S246 Oh 2022 (print)
| LCC PZ7.7.S246 (ebook) |DDC 741.5/973—dc23
LC record available at https://lccn.loc.gov/2021053464
LC ebook record available at https://lccn.loc.gov/2021053465

SPRINKLES AND SWIRLS

Oh, What a Show!

Written by **LOLA M. SCHAEFER** ★ Illustrated by **SAVANNAH ALLEN**

Ready-to-Read *GRAPHICS*

Simon Spotlight
New York   London   Toronto   Sydney   New Delhi

HOW TO READ THIS BOOK

Sprinkles and Swirls are here to give you some tips on reading this book.

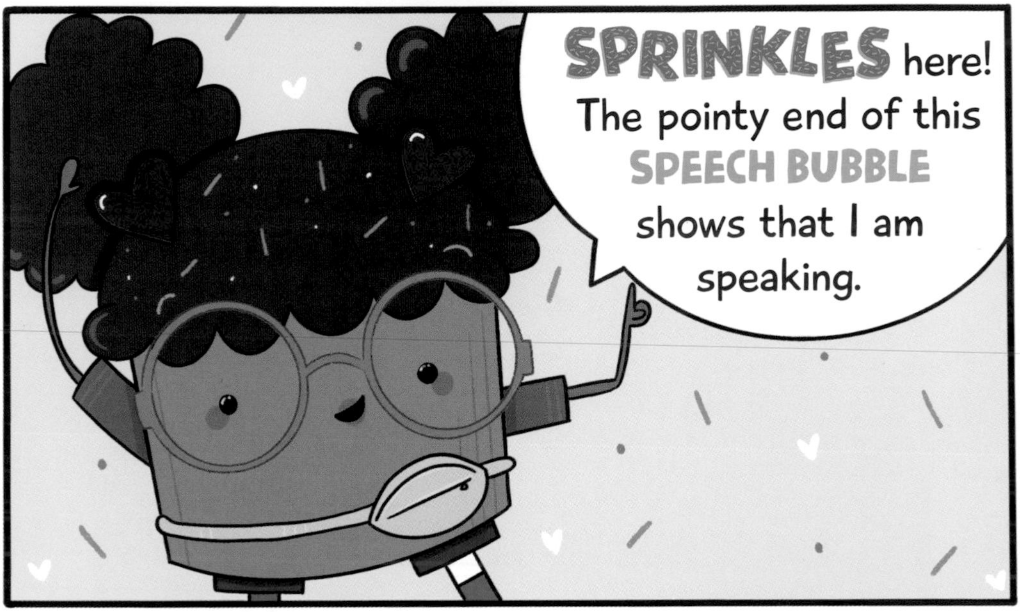
SPRINKLES here! The pointy end of this SPEECH BUBBLE shows that I am speaking.

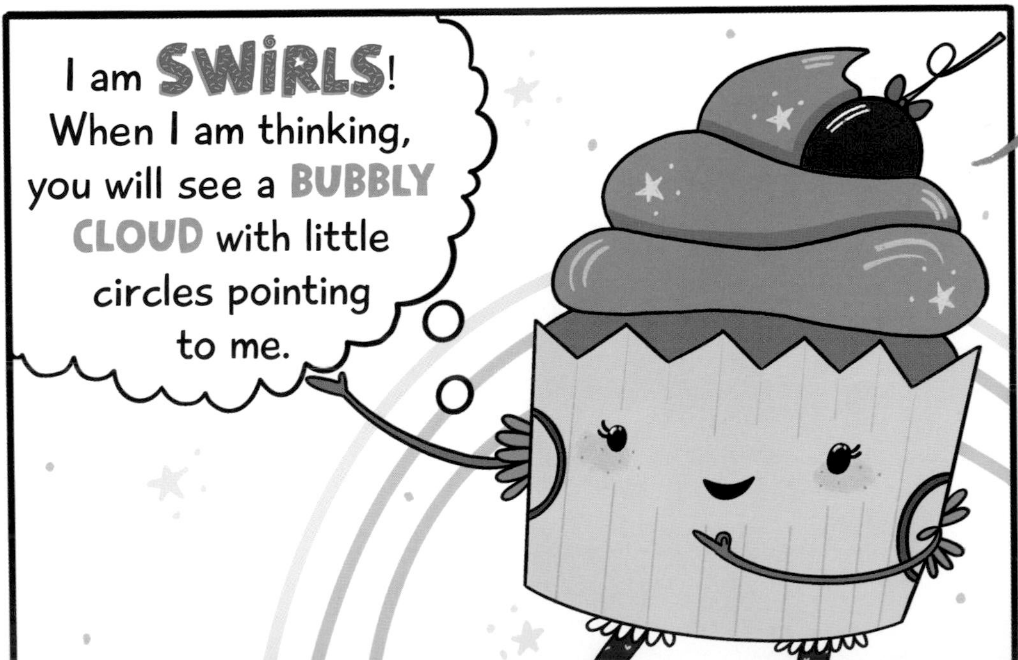
I am SWIRLS! When I am thinking, you will see a BUBBLY CLOUD with little circles pointing to me.

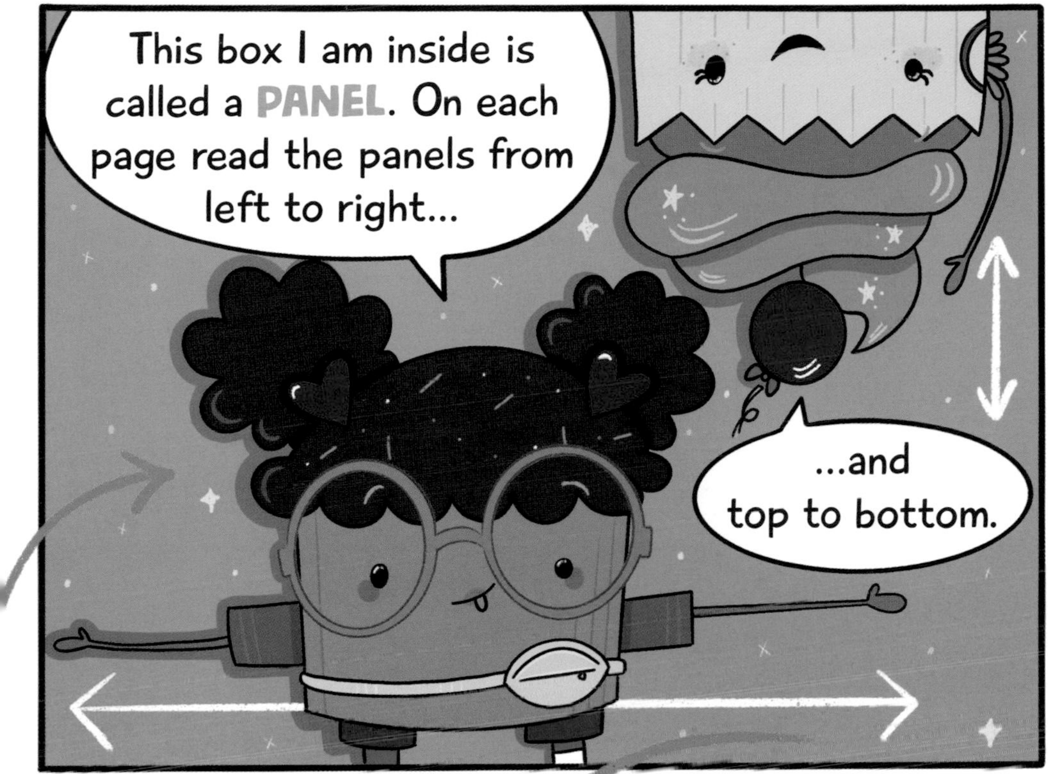
This box I am inside is called a PANEL. On each page read the panels from left to right...
...and top to bottom.

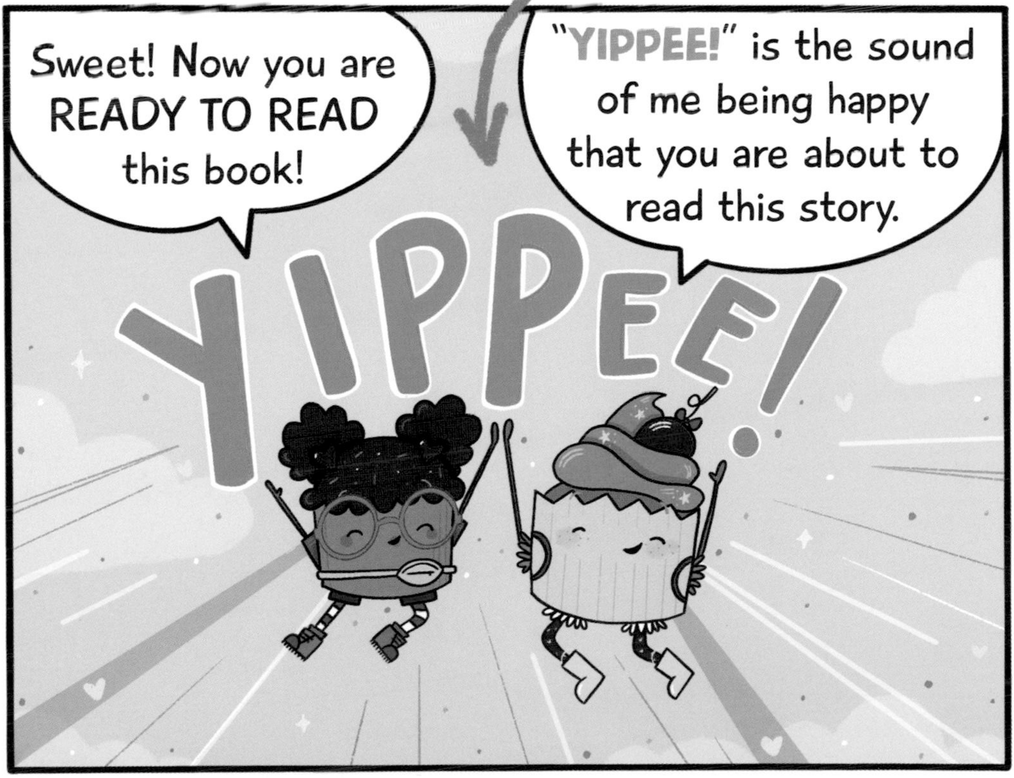
Sweet! Now you are READY TO READ this book!
"YIPPEE!" is the sound of me being happy that you are about to read this story.
YIPPEE!

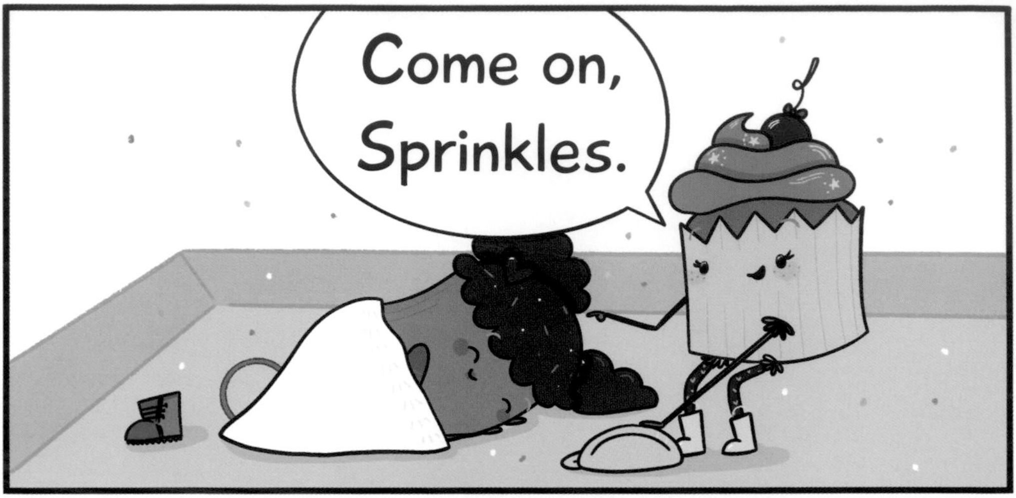
Come on, Sprinkles.

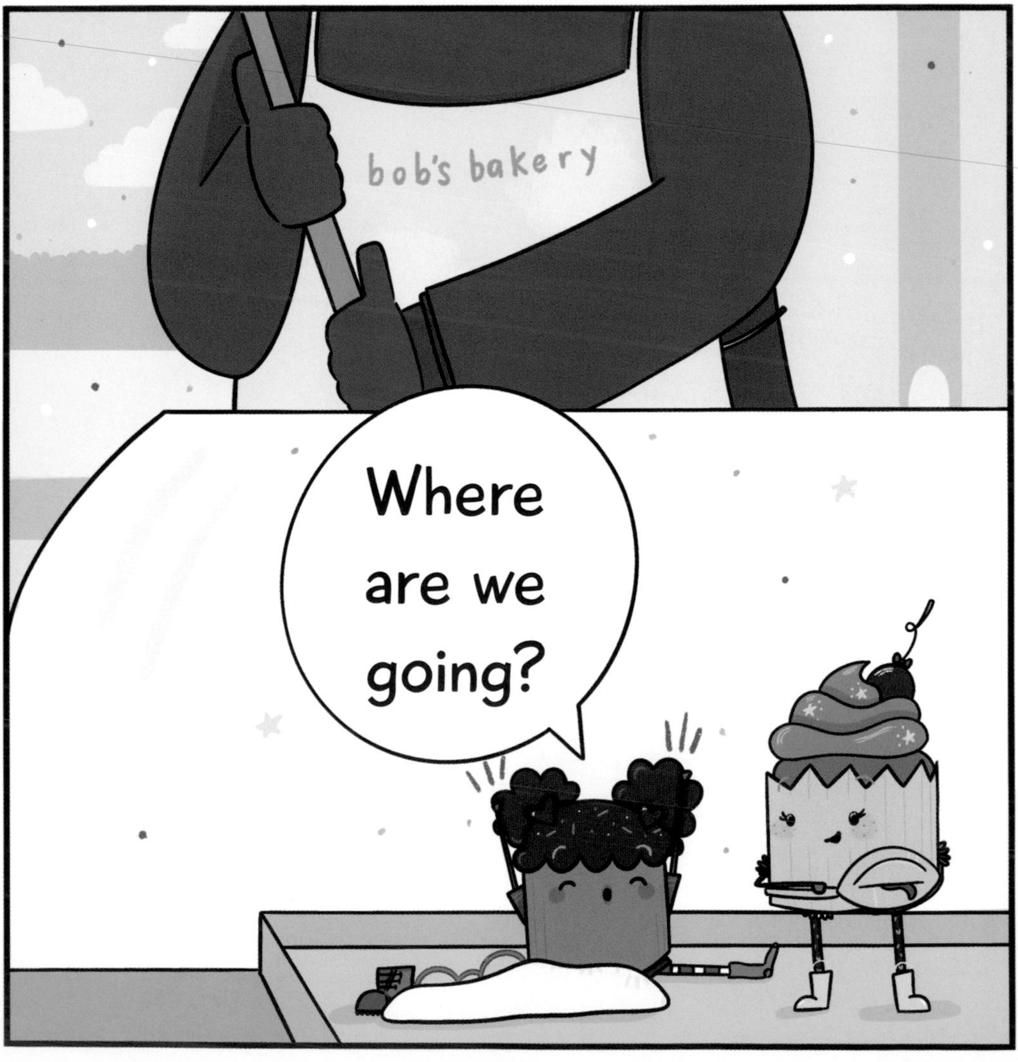
bob's bakery
Where are we going?

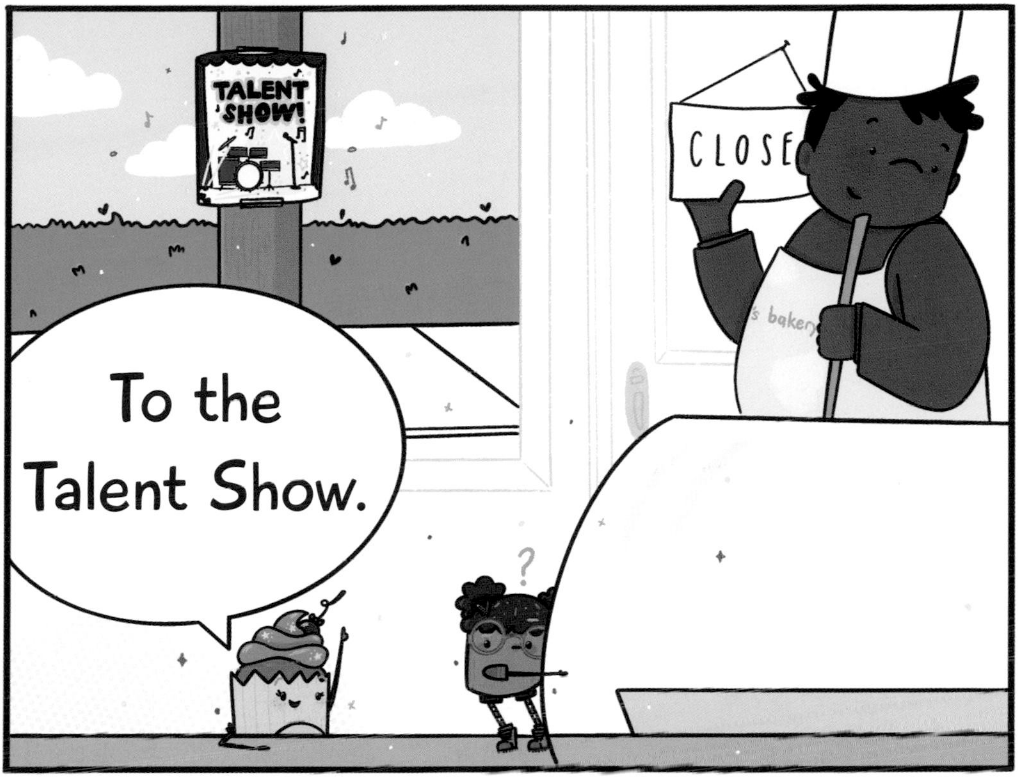
TALENT SHOW!
CLOSE
bakery
To the Talent Show.
?

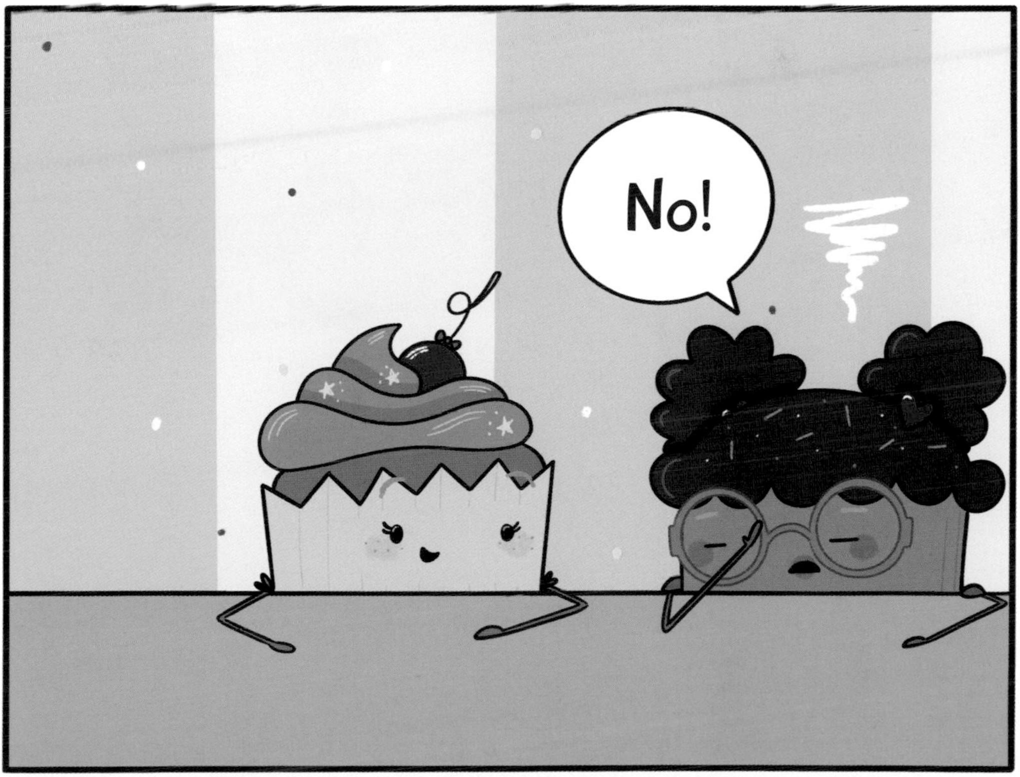
No!

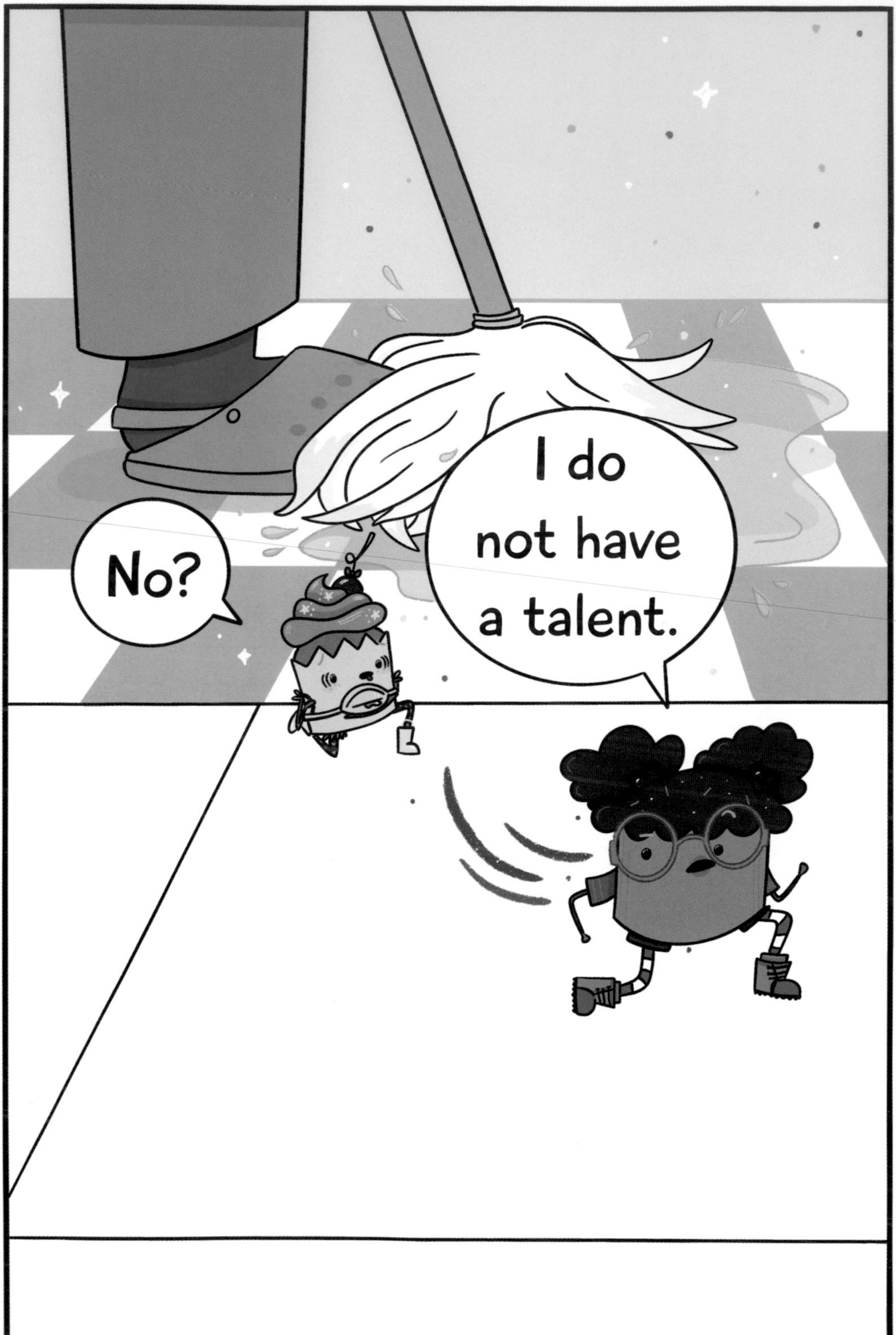
No?
I do not have a talent.

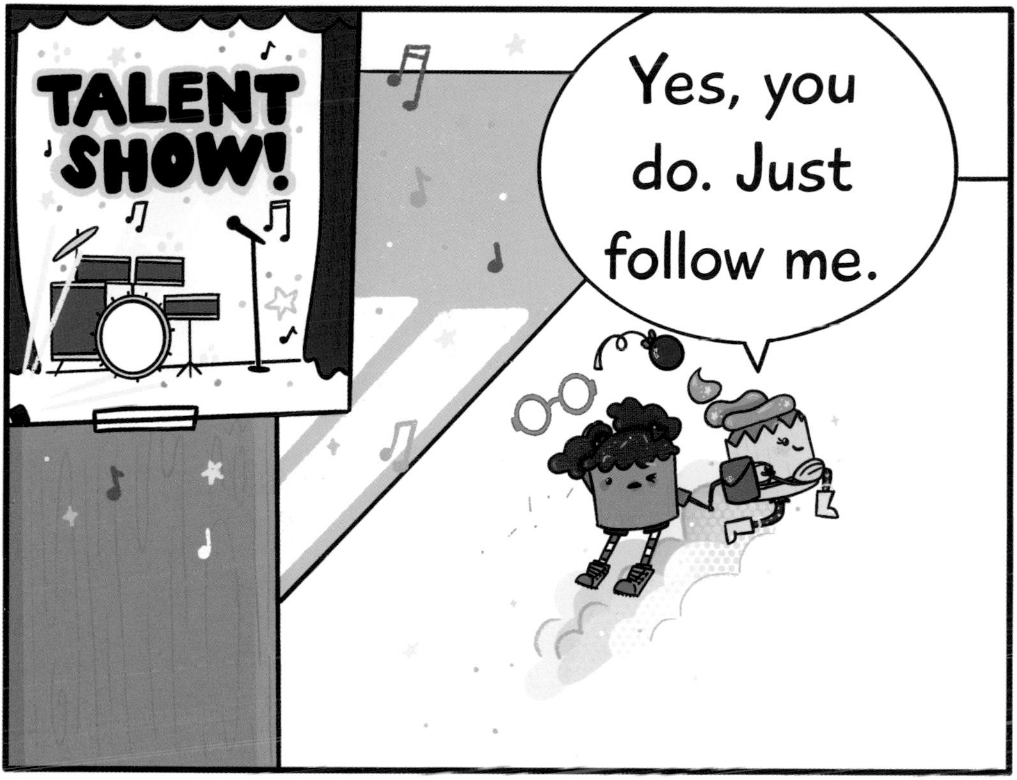
TALENT SHOW!
Yes, you do. Just follow me.

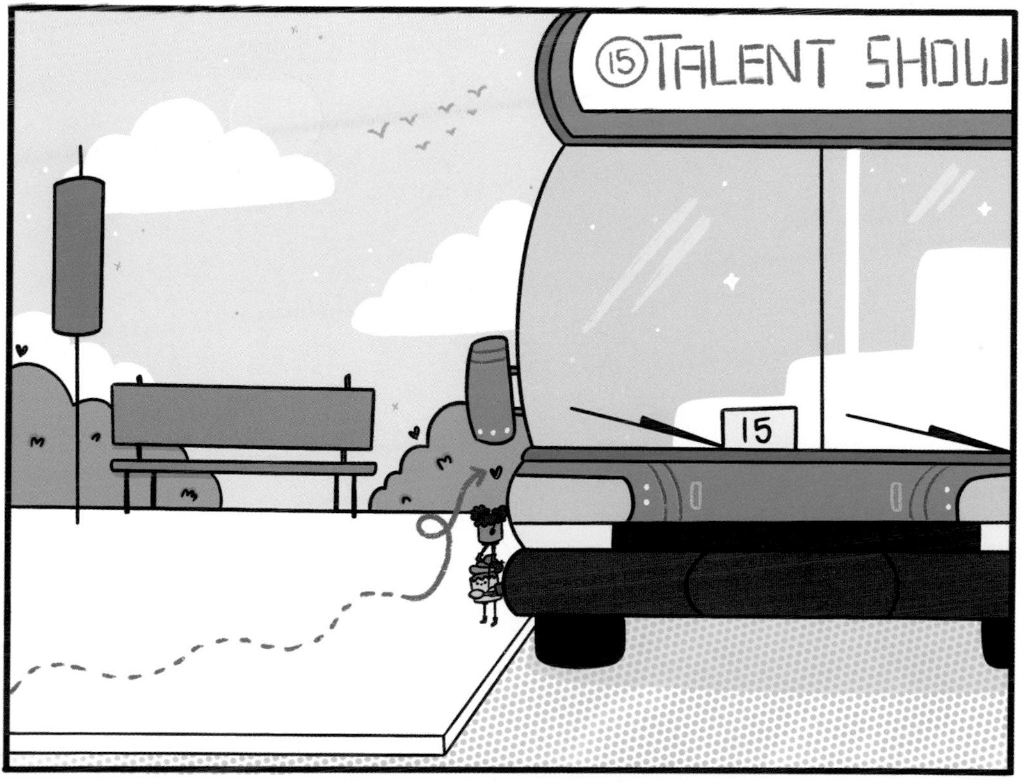
15 TALENT SHOW
15

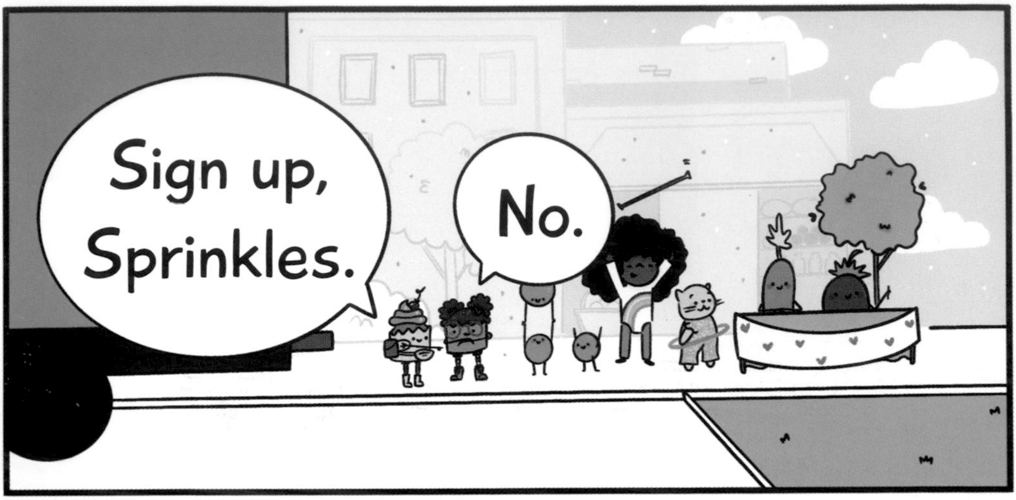
Sign up, Sprinkles.
No.

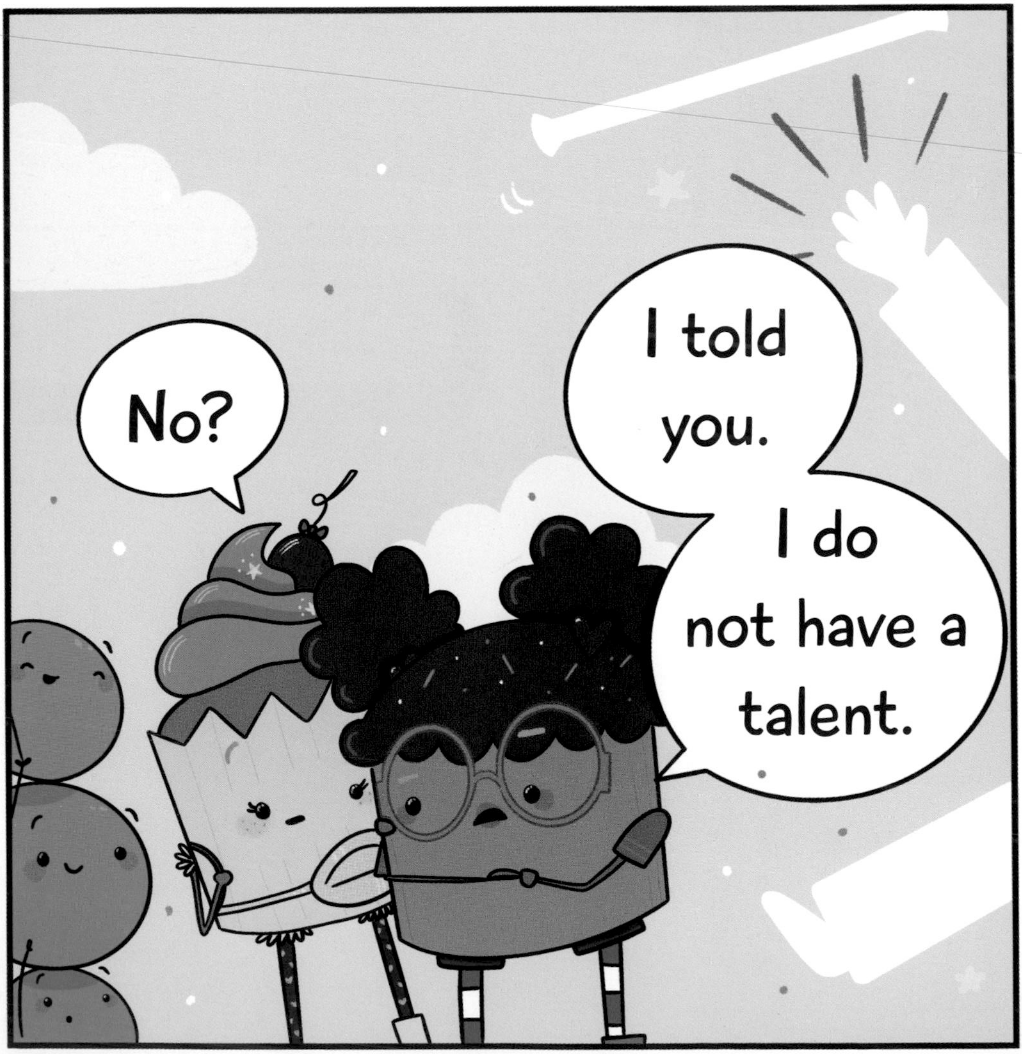
No?
I told you.
I do not have a talent.

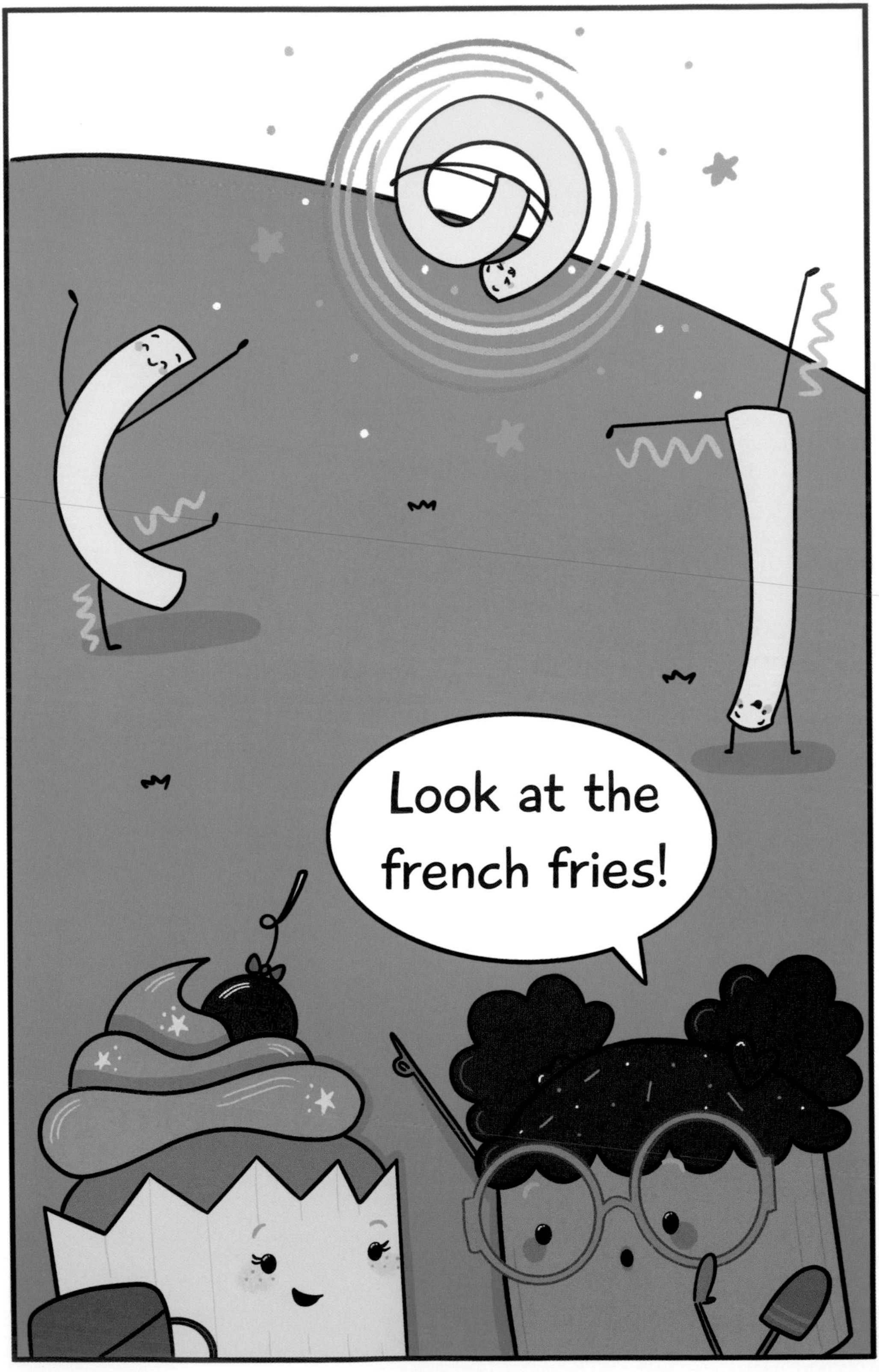
Look at the french fries!

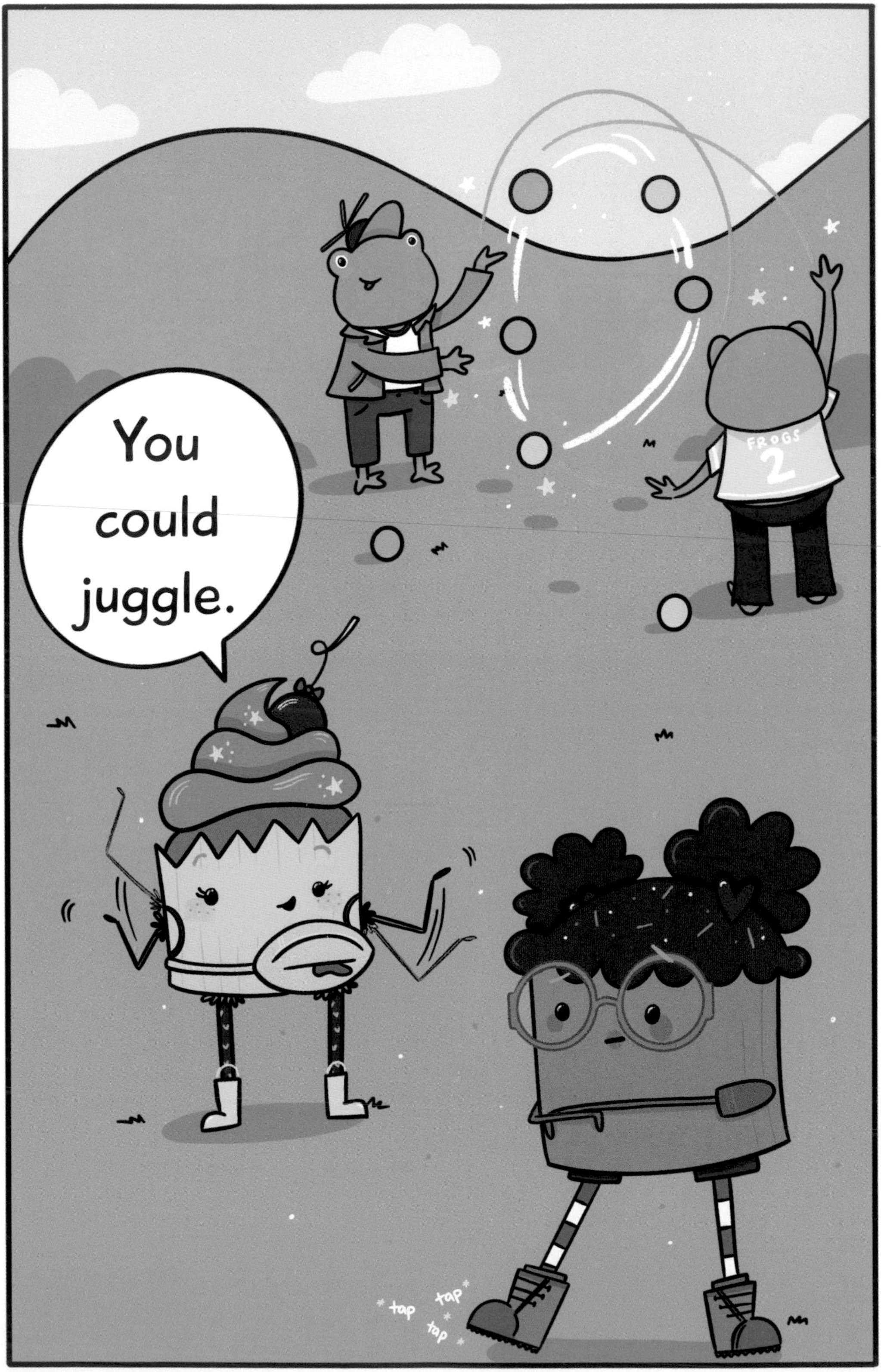
You could juggle.
FROGS 2
tap tap tap

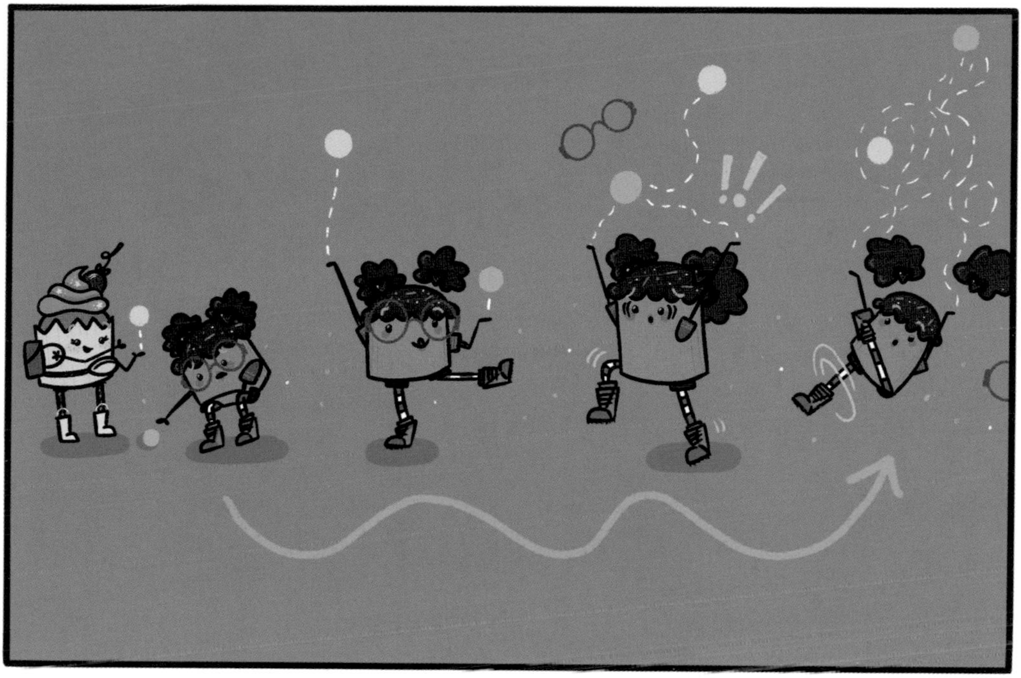

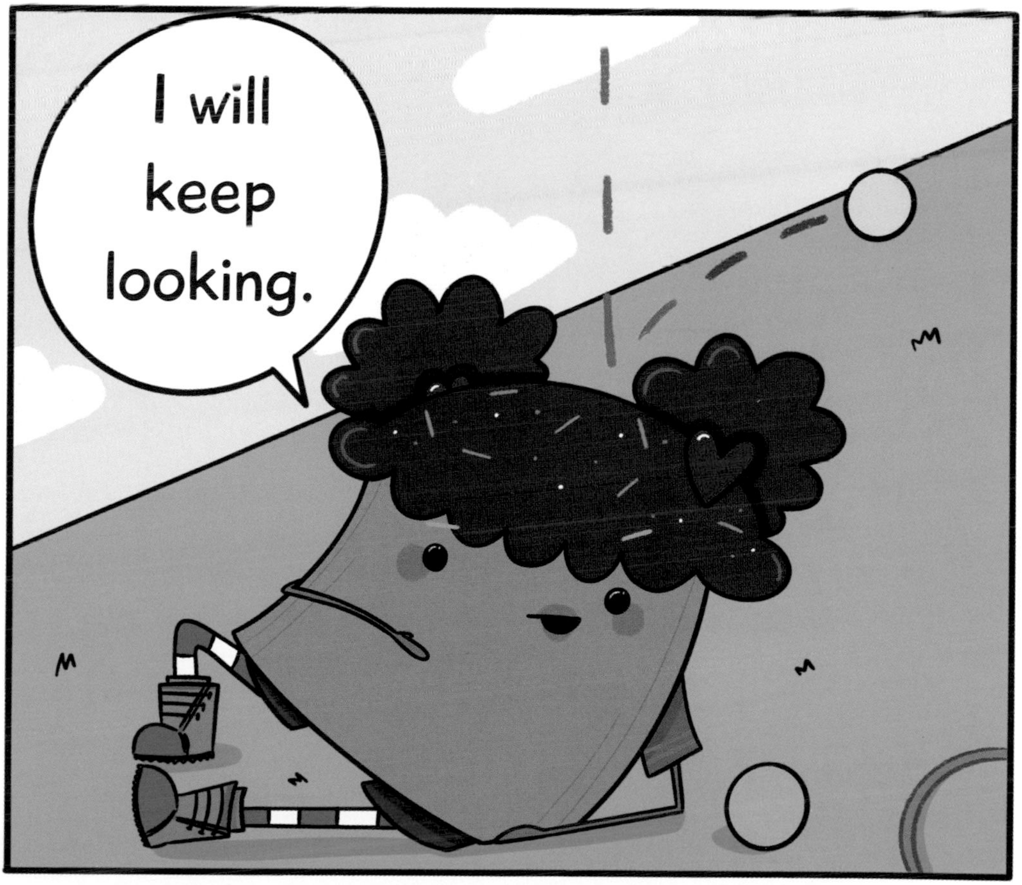
I will keep looking.

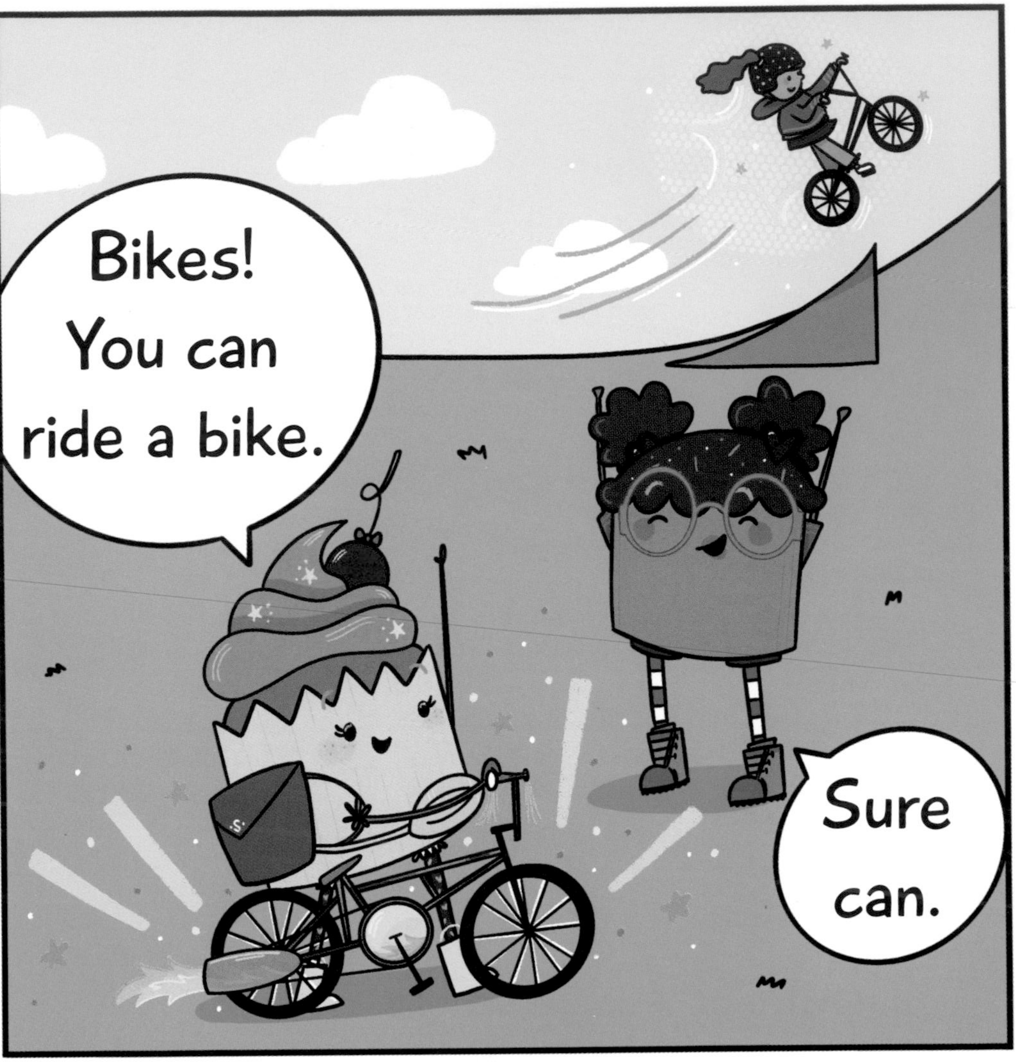
Bikes! You can ride a bike.
Sure can.

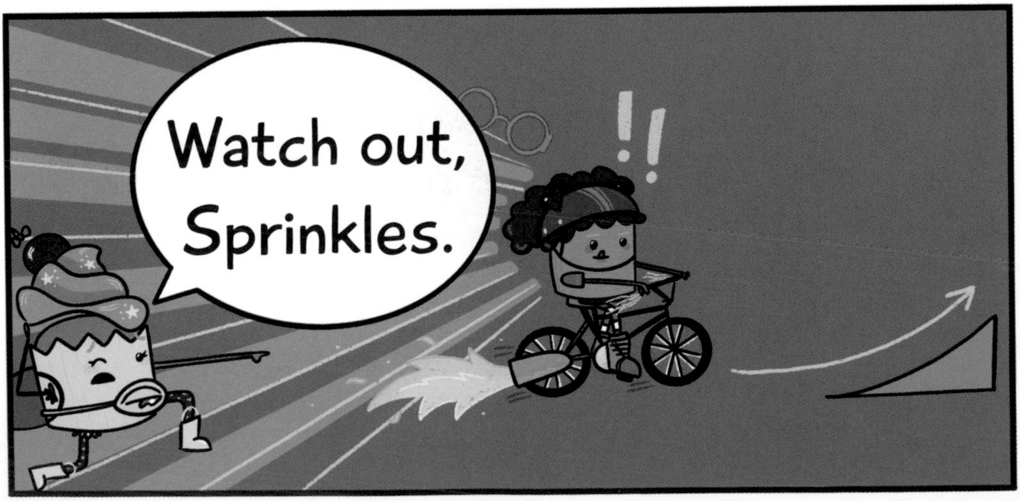
Watch out, Sprinkles.
!!

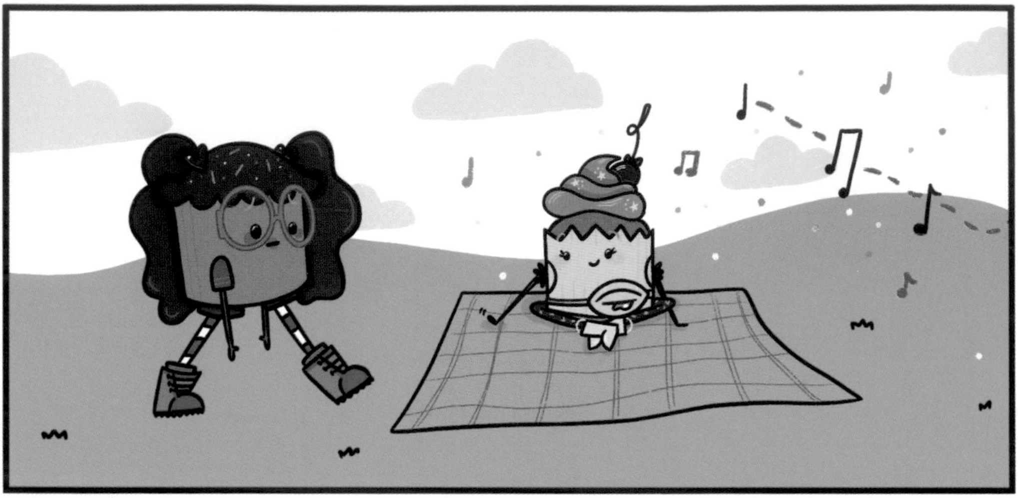

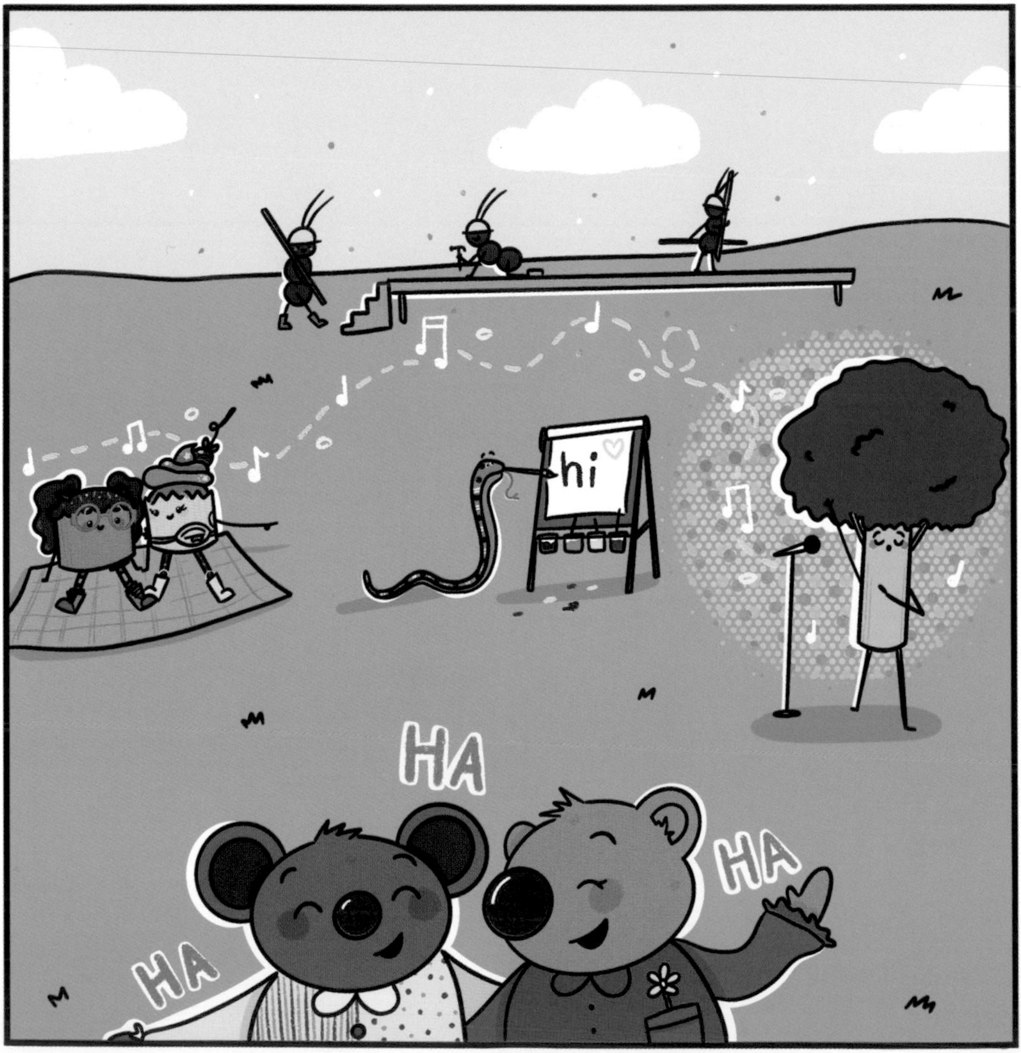
hi
HA
HA
HA

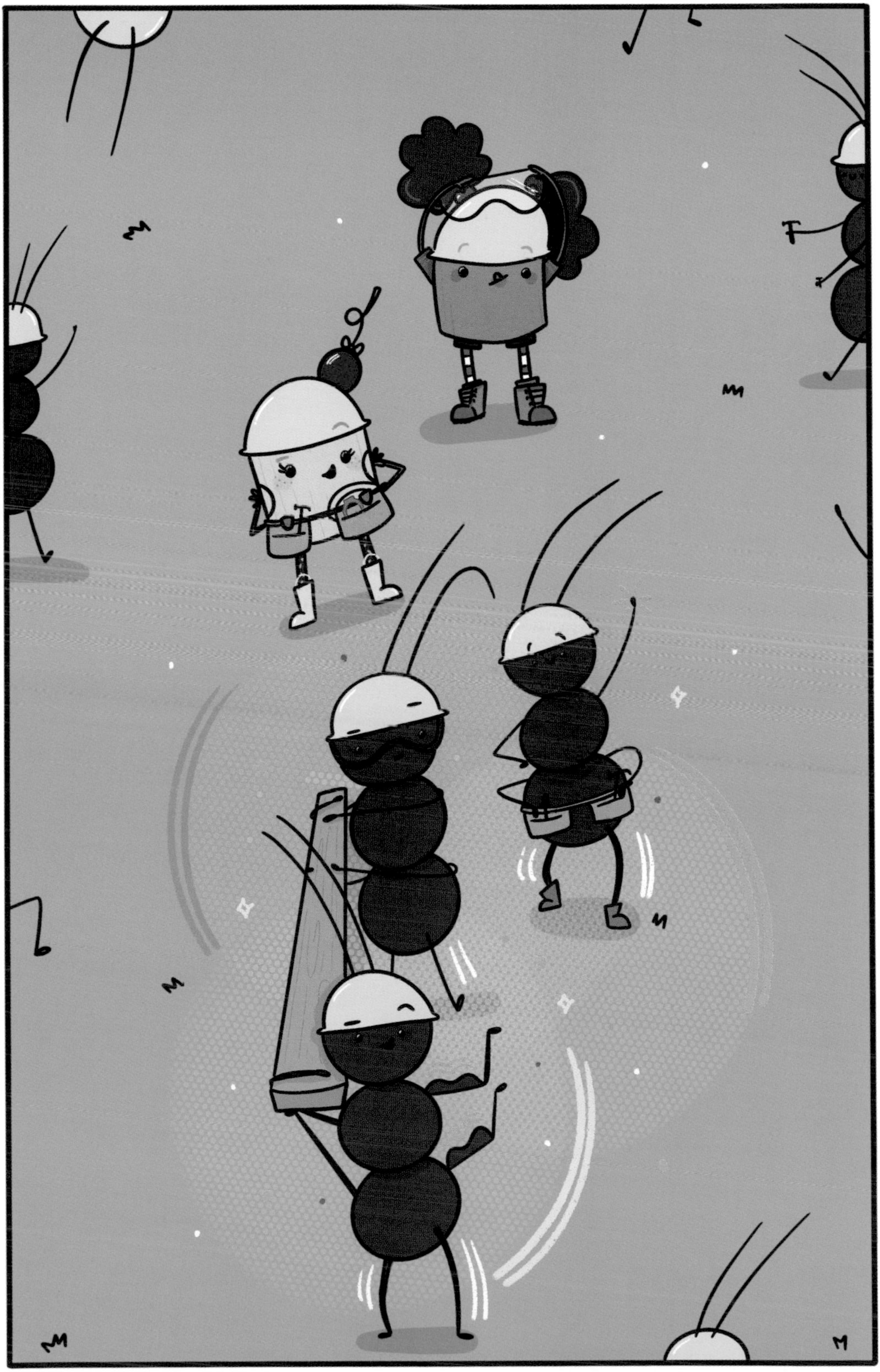

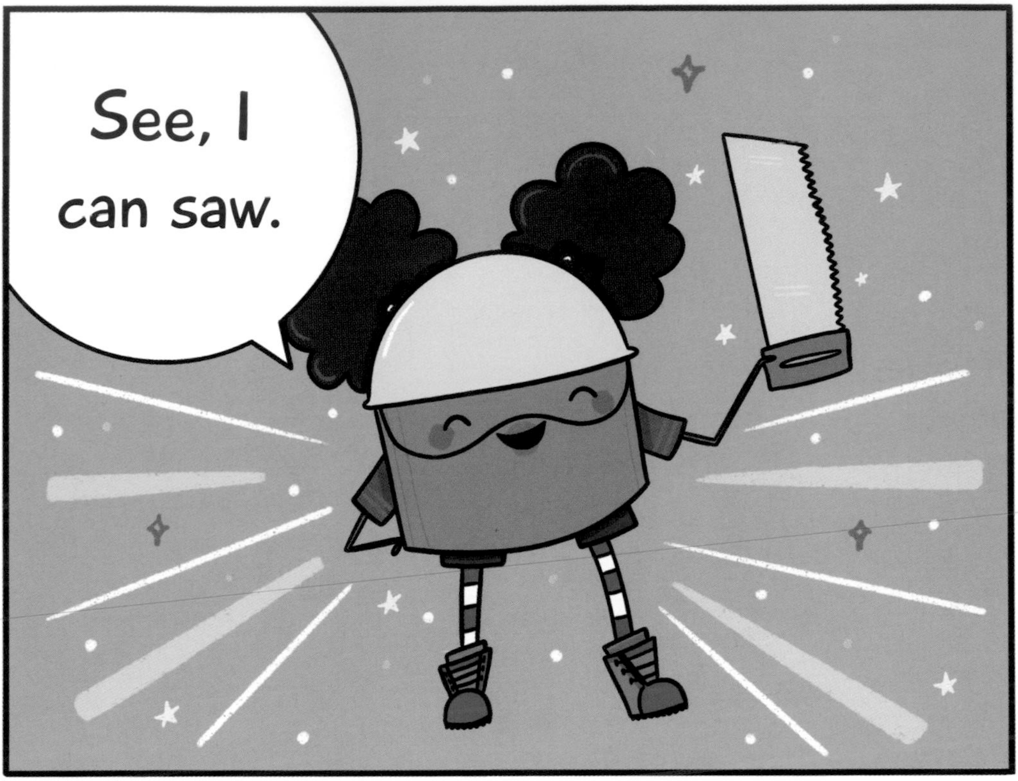
See, I can saw.

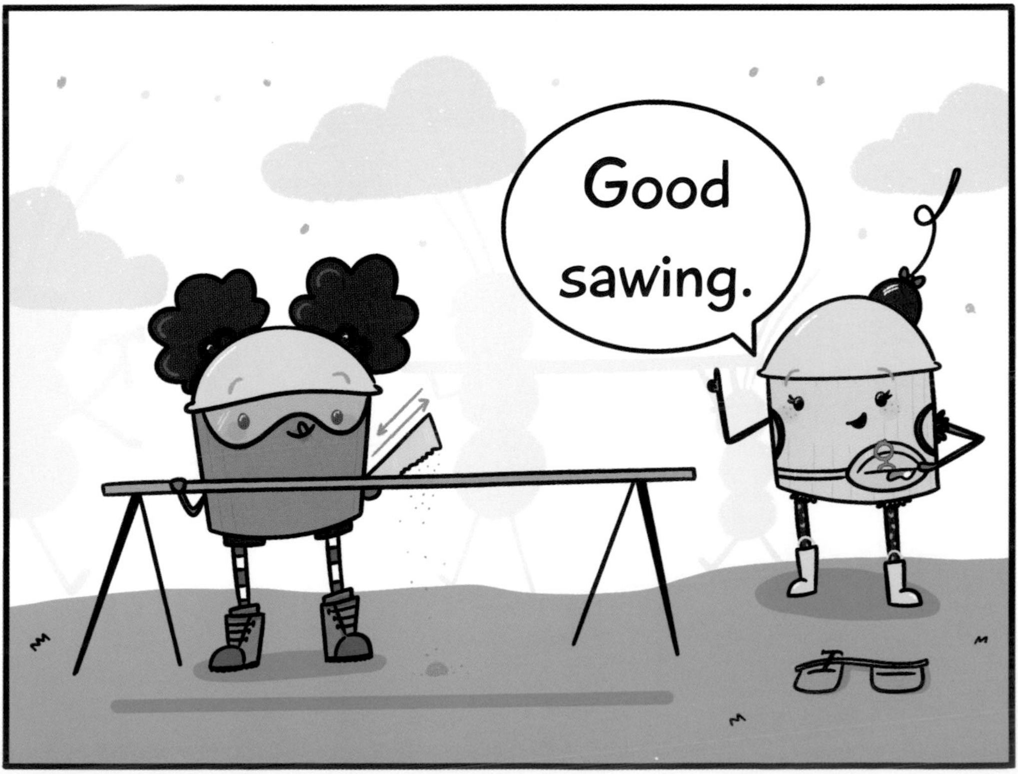
Good sawing.

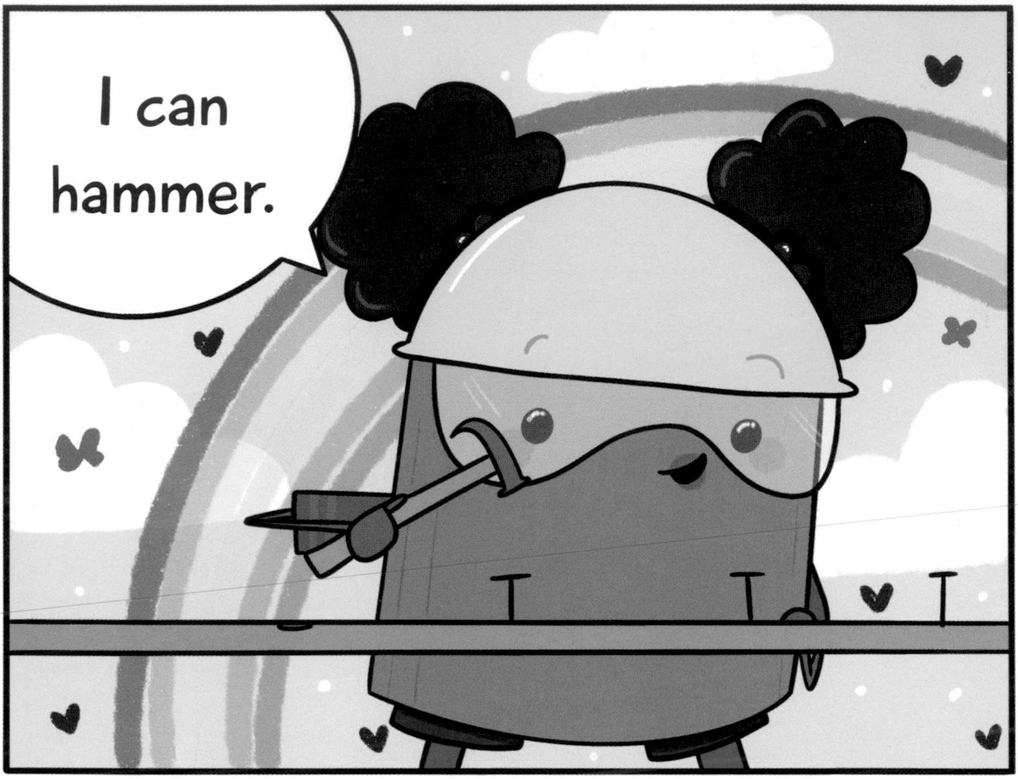
I can hammer.

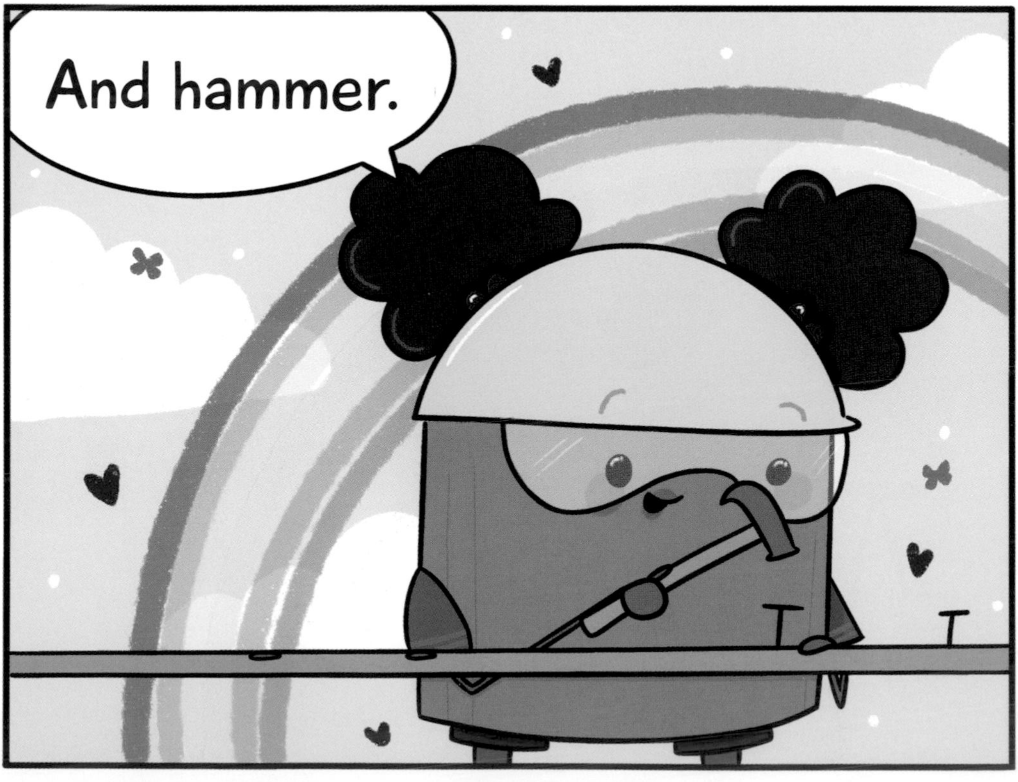
And hammer.

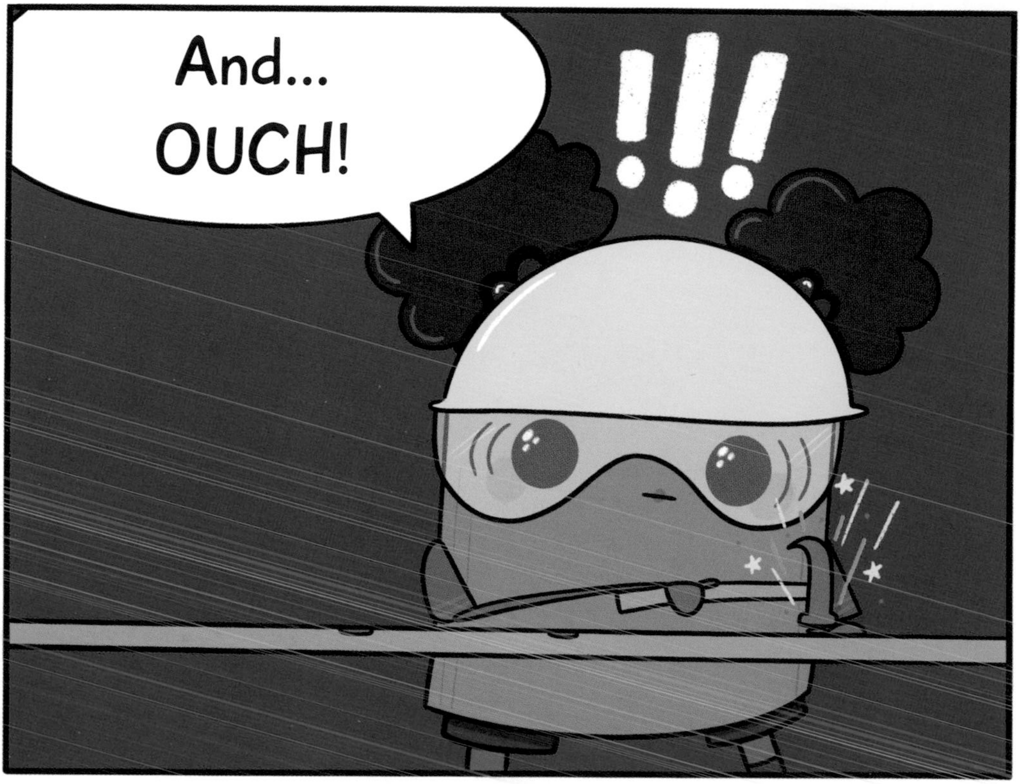
And...
OUCH!
!!!

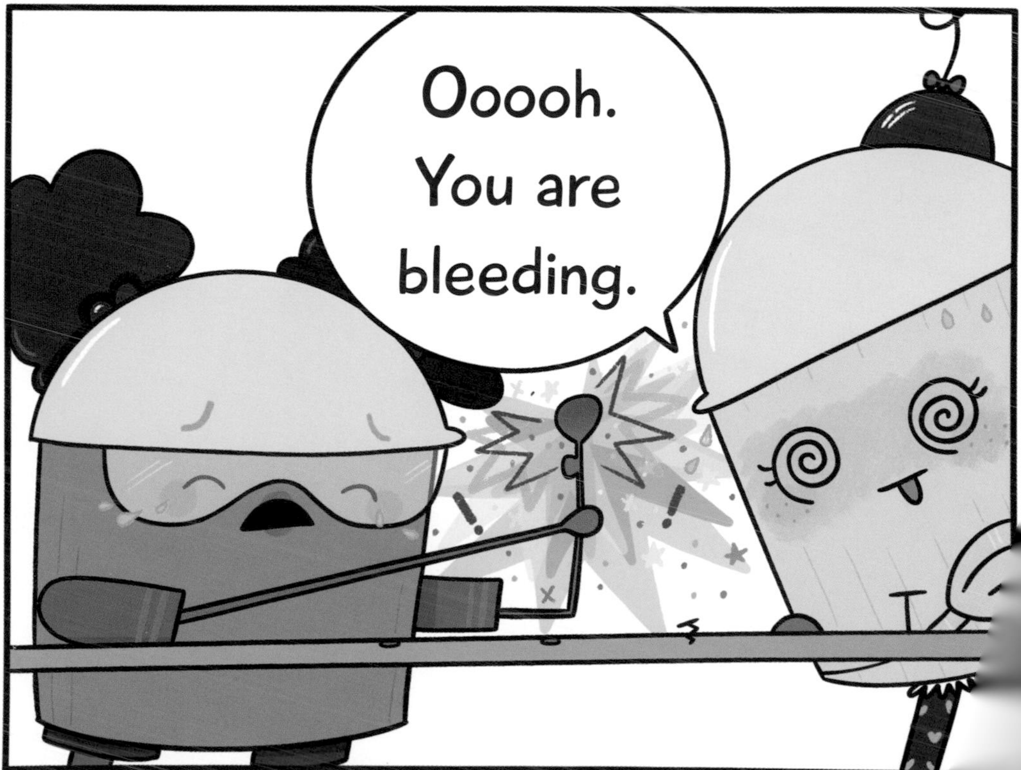
Ooooh.
You are
bleeding.

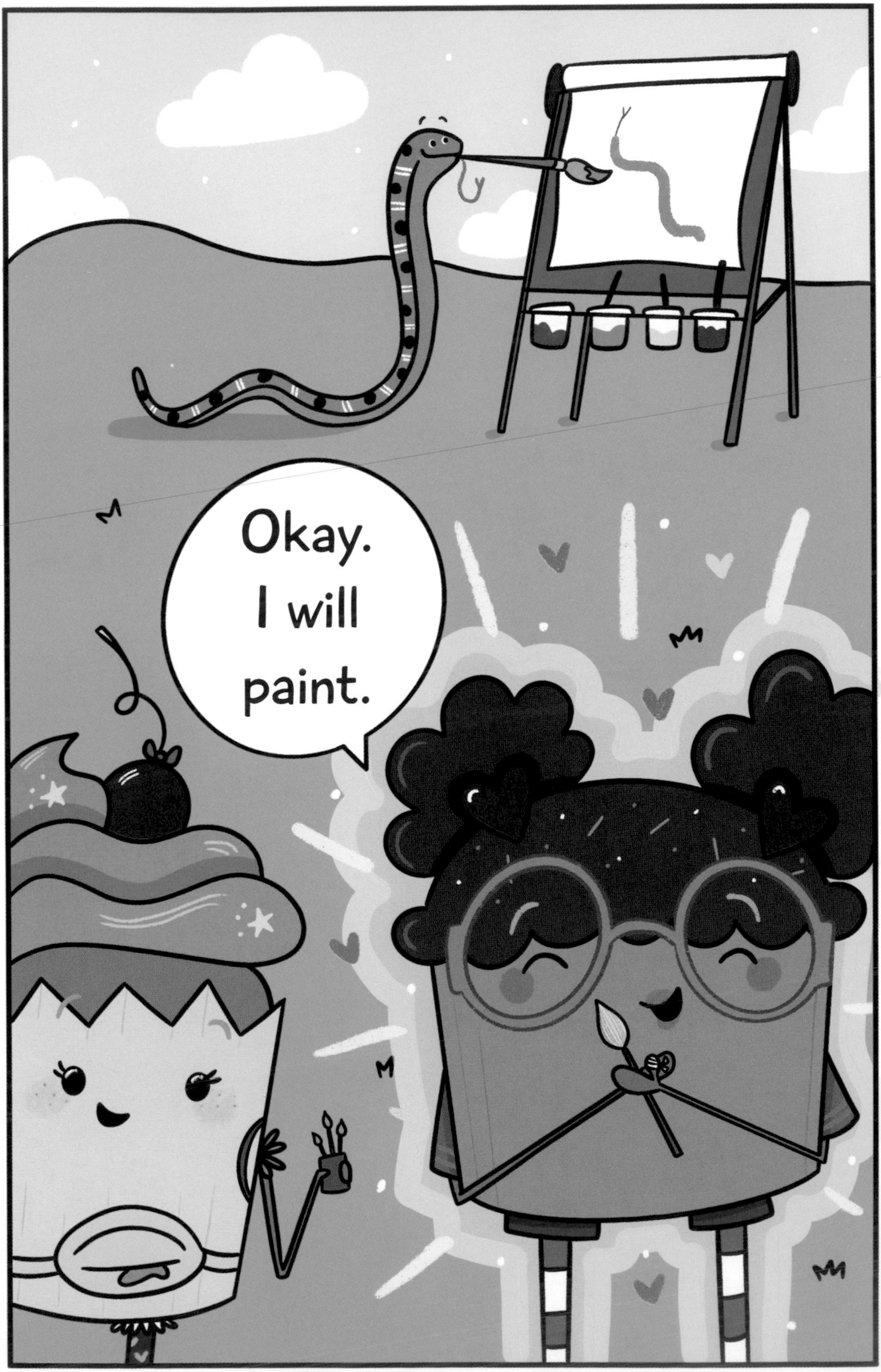
Okay. I will paint.

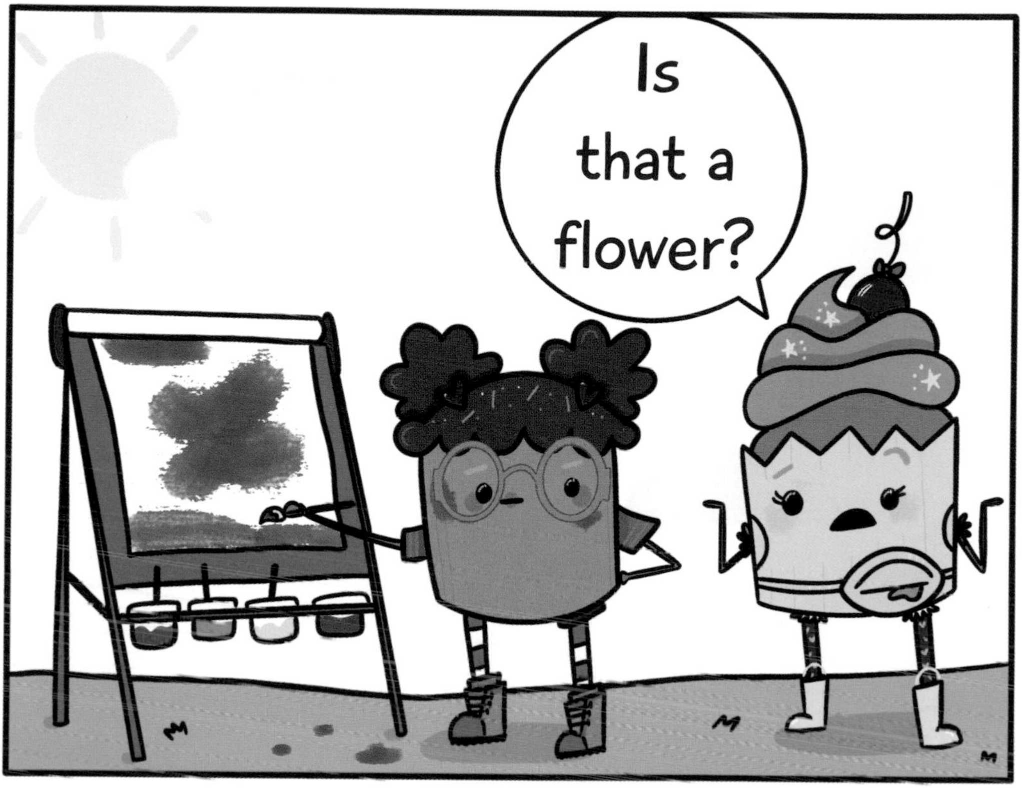
Is that a flower?

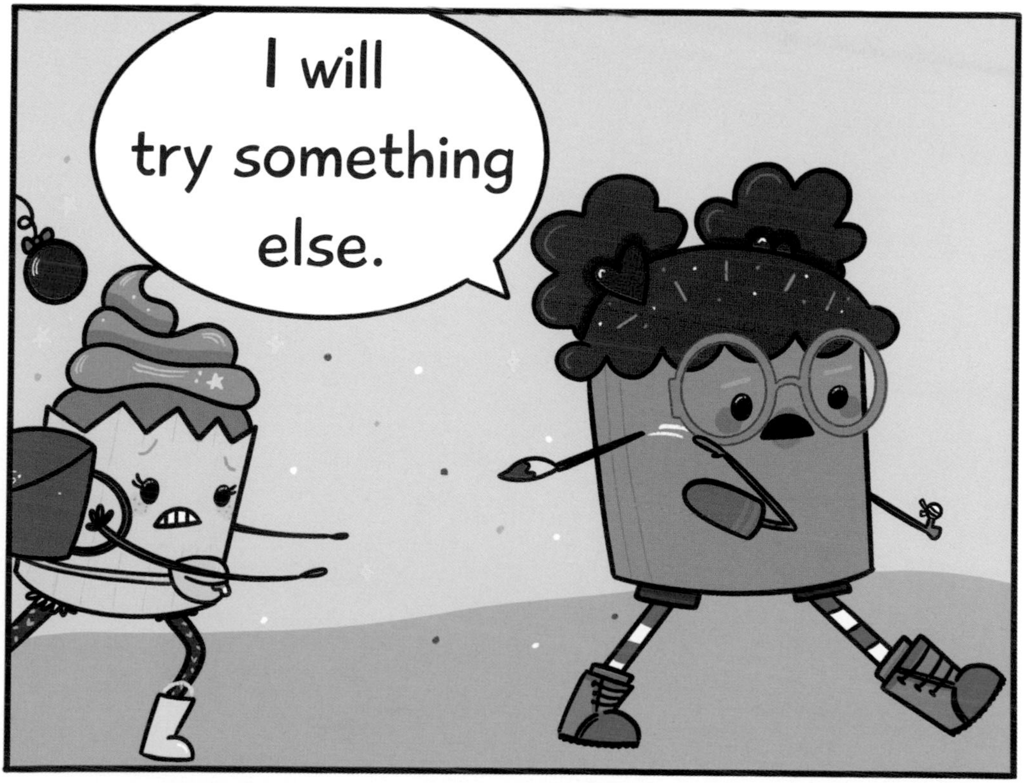
I will try something else.

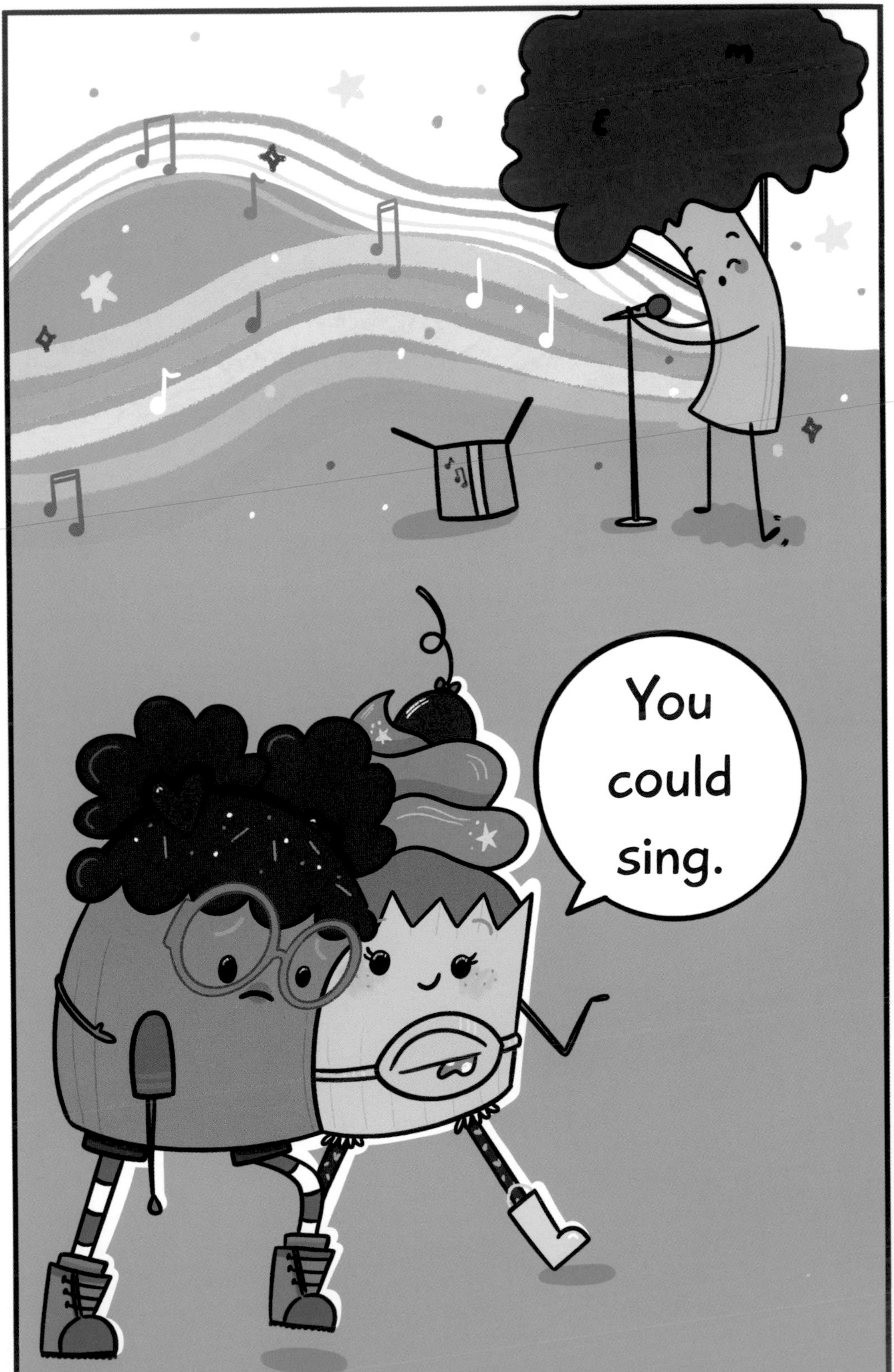
You could sing.

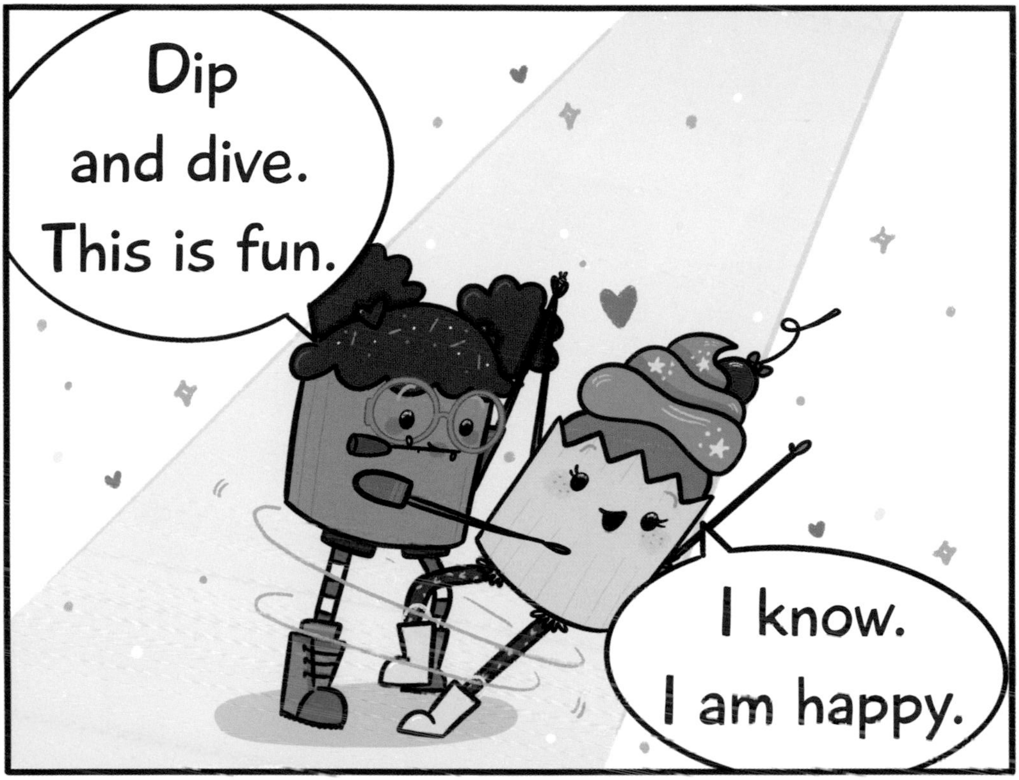
Dip and dive. This is fun.
I know. I am happy.

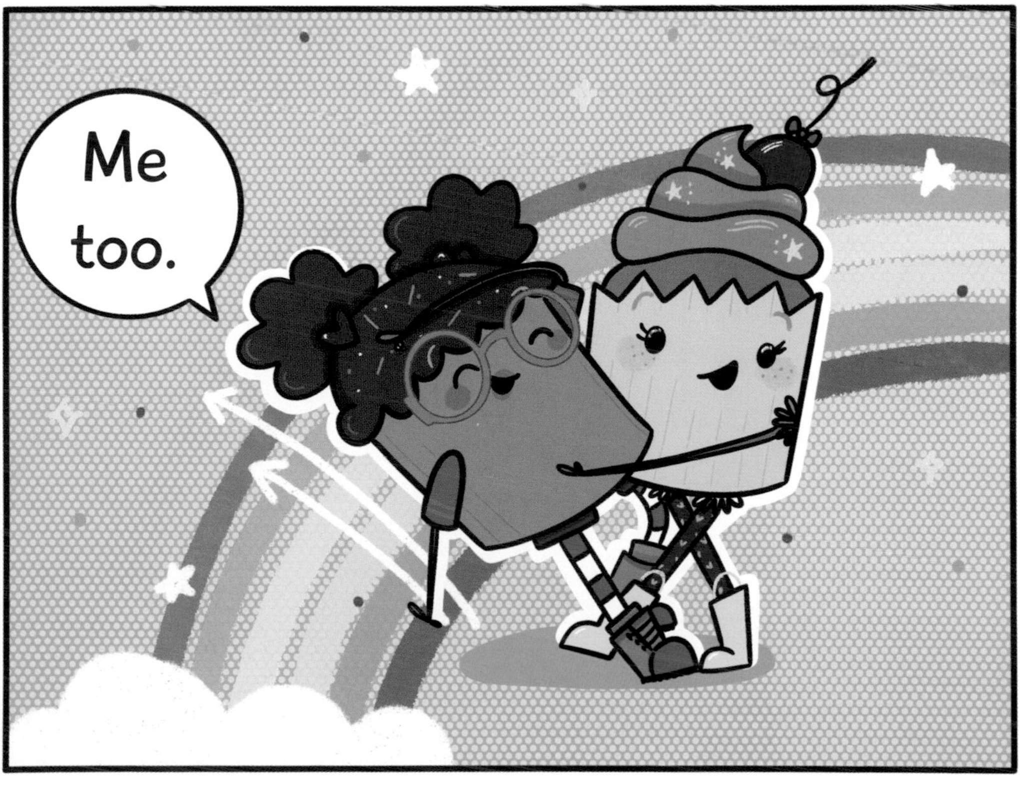
Me too.

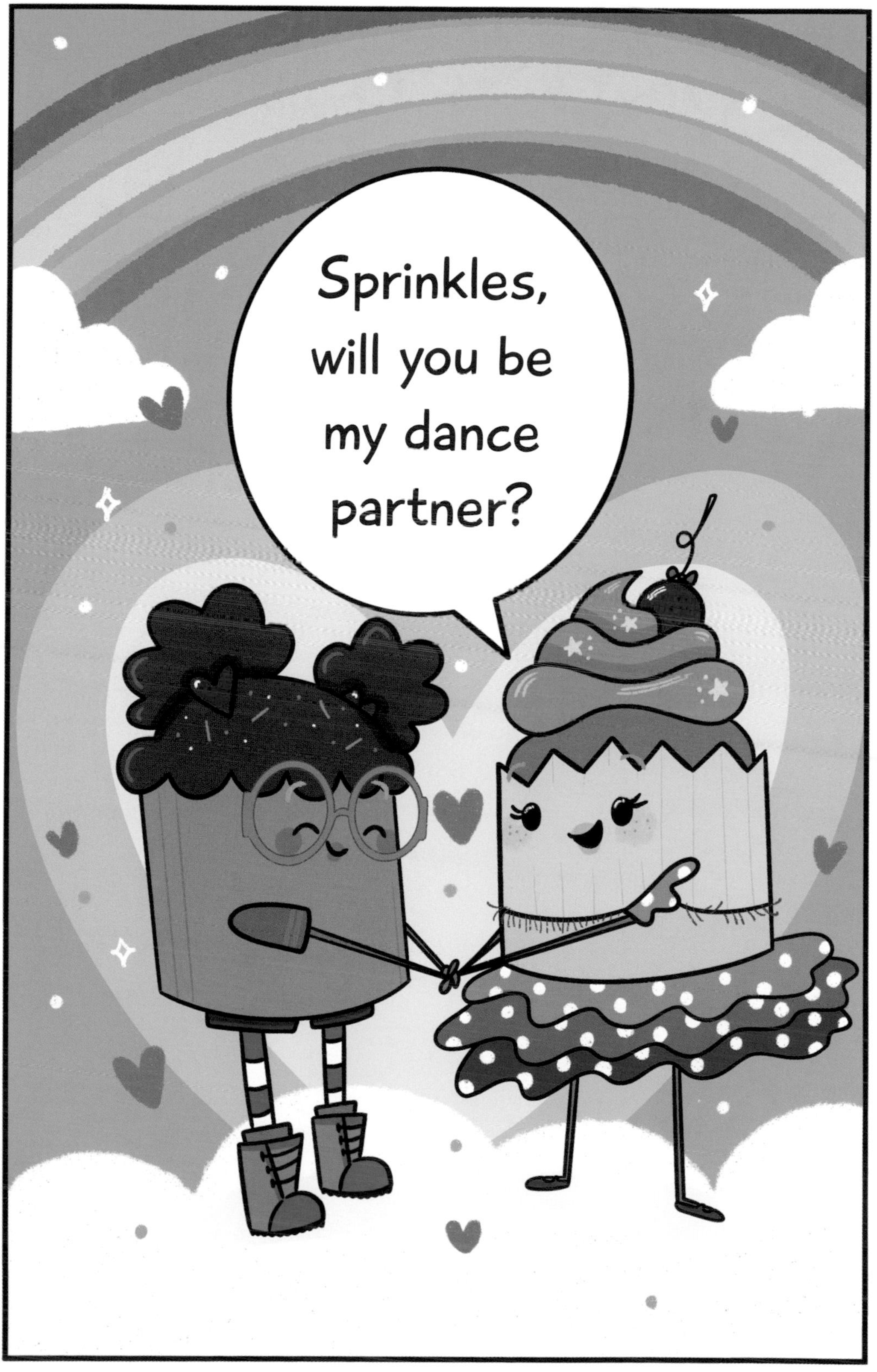
Sprinkles, will you be my dance partner?

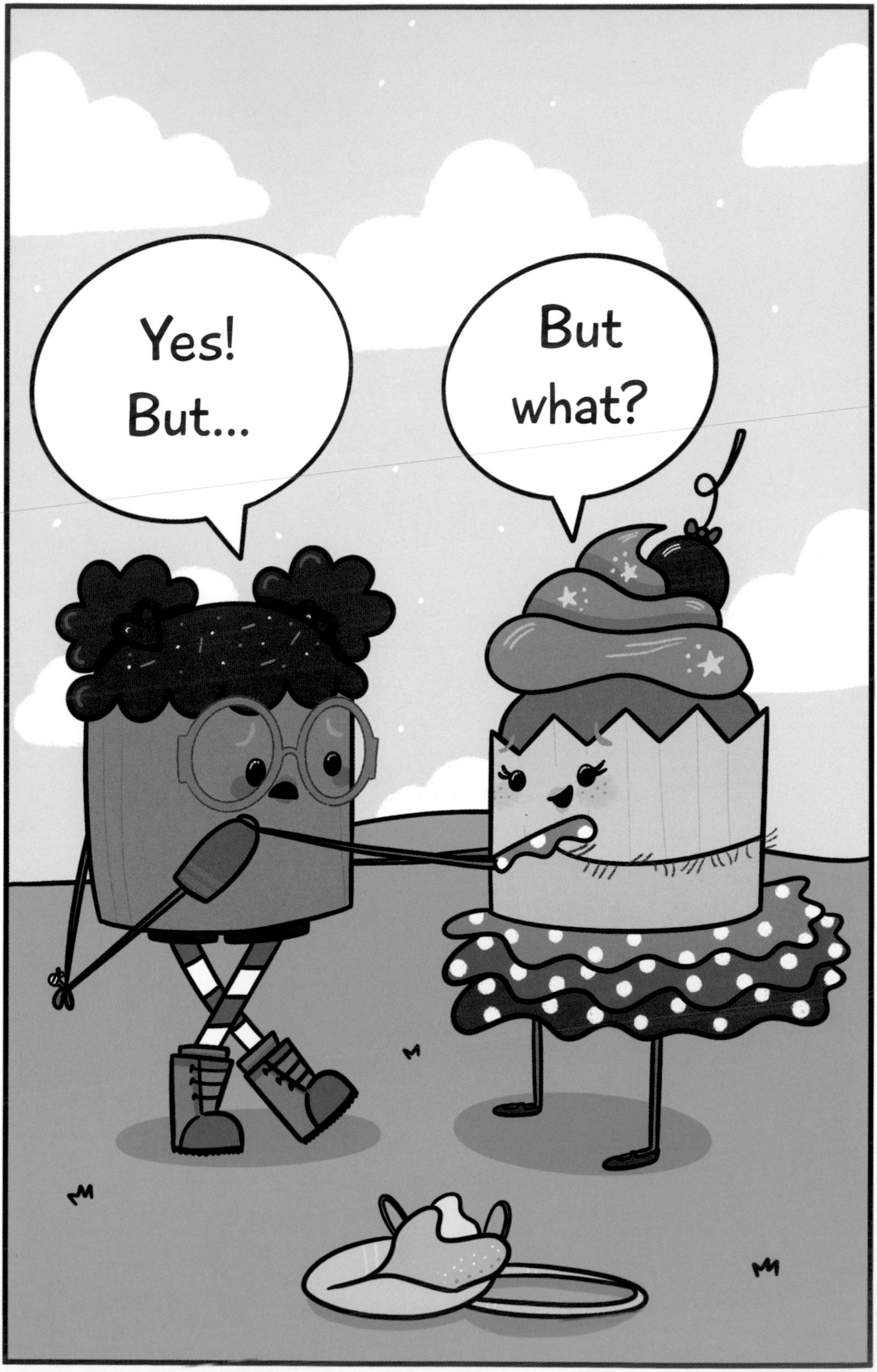
Yes! But...
But what?

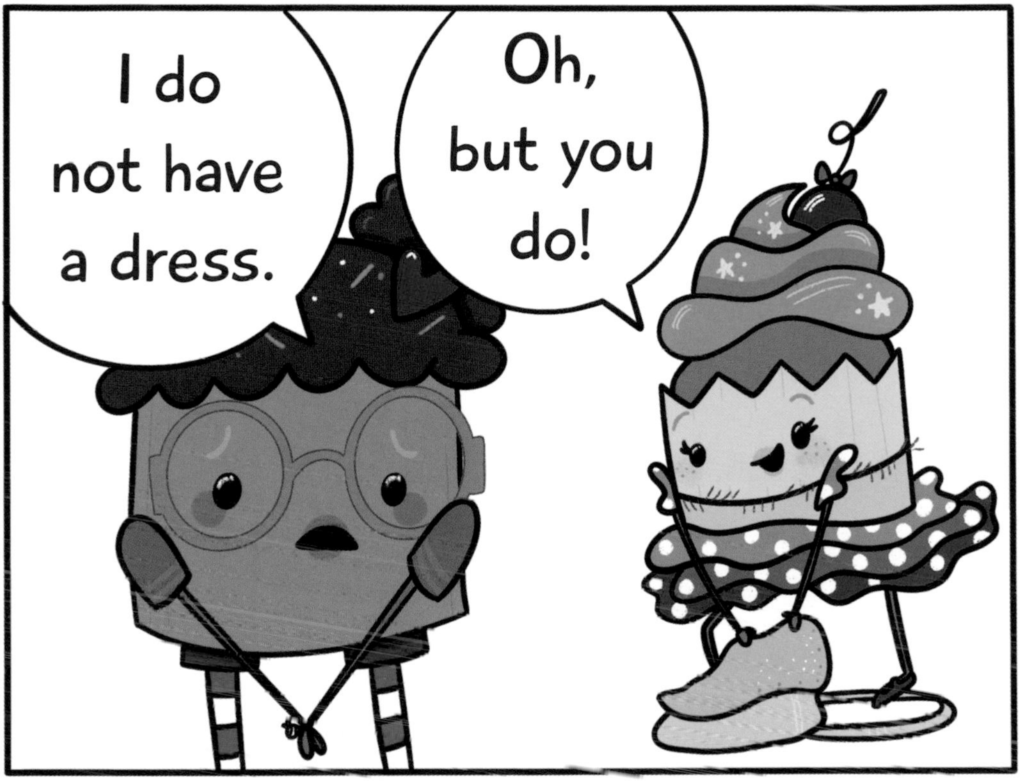
I do not have a dress.
Oh, but you do!

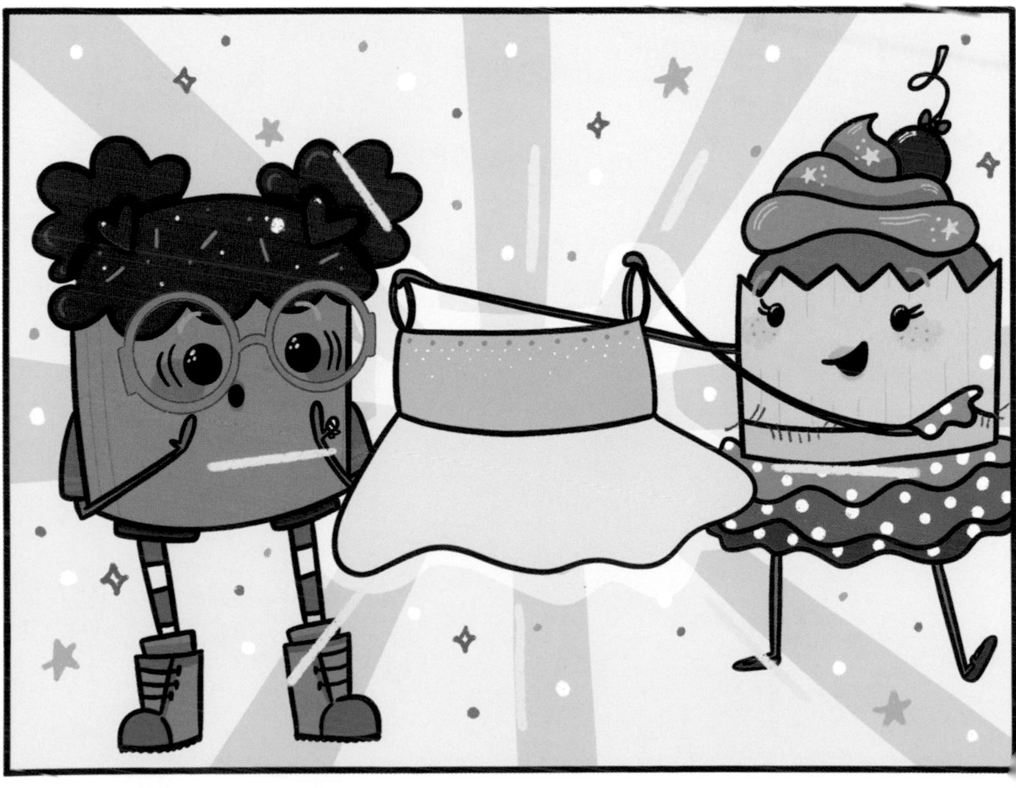

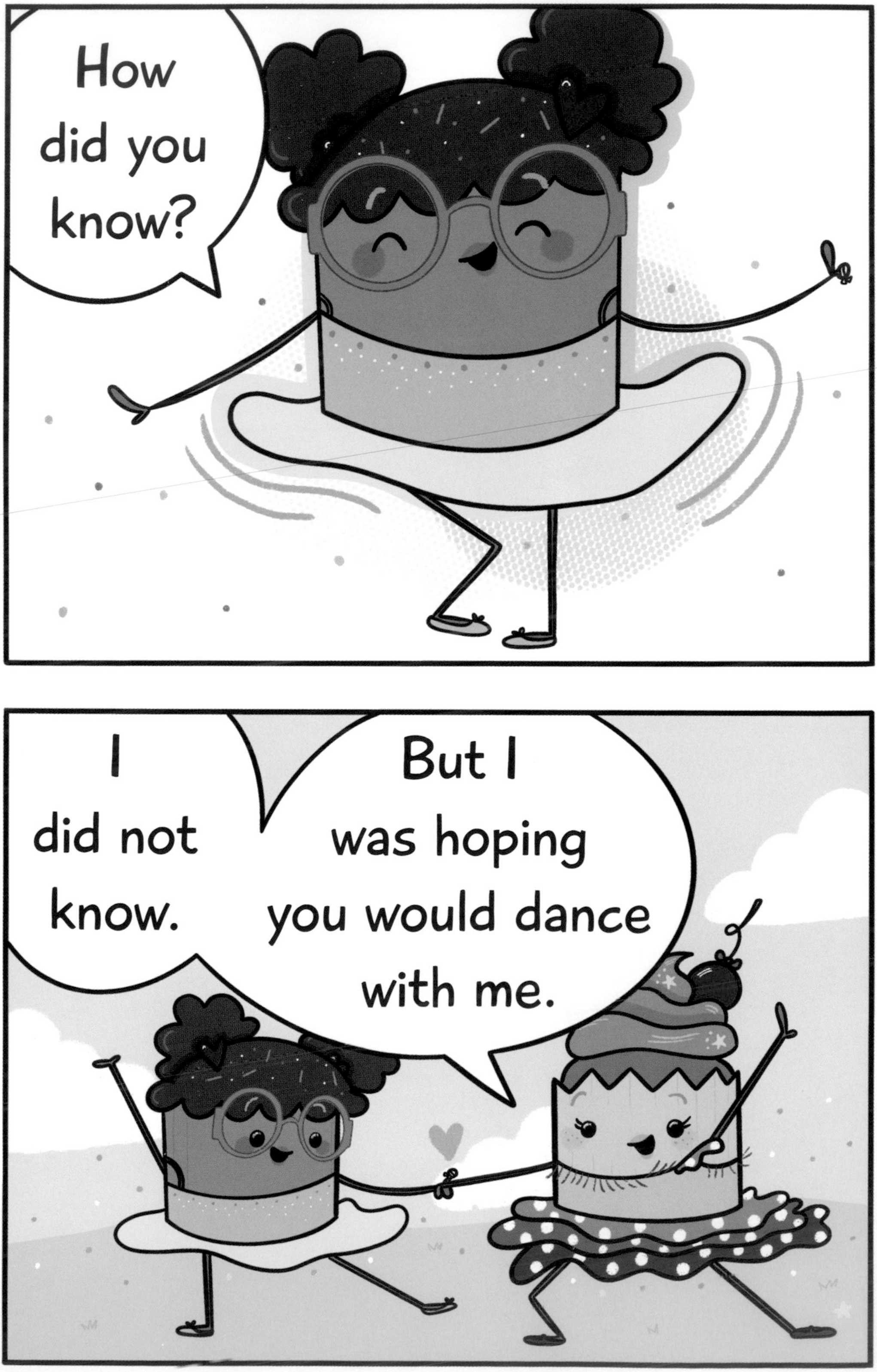
How did you know?
I did not know.
But I was hoping you would dance with me.

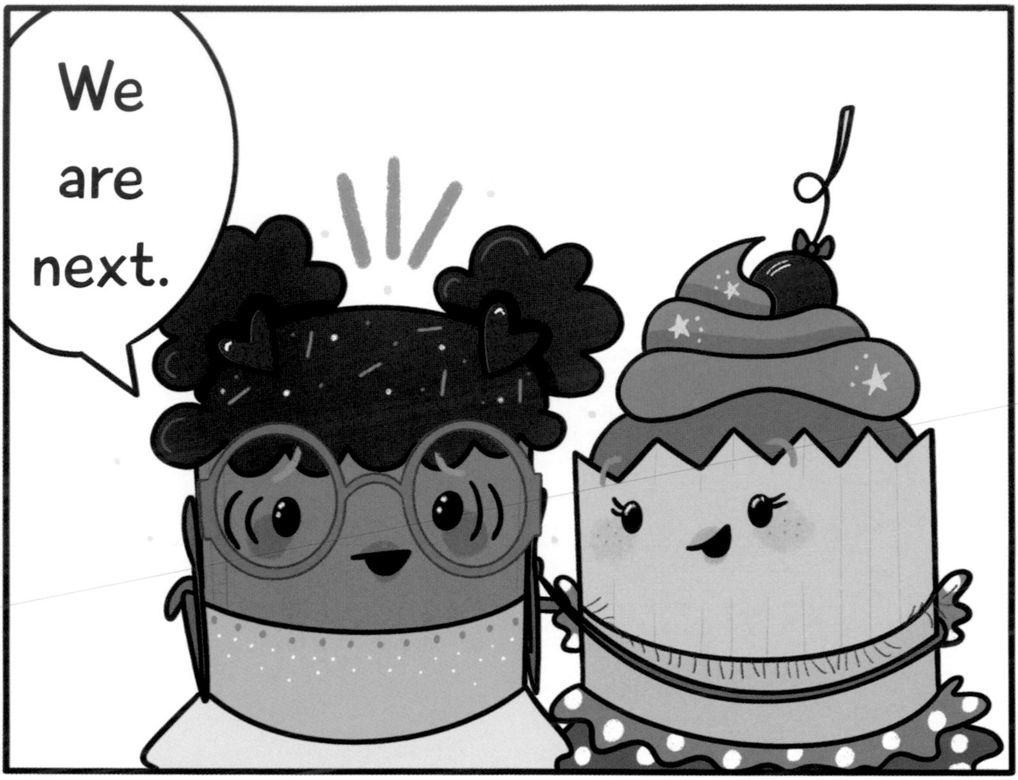
We are next.

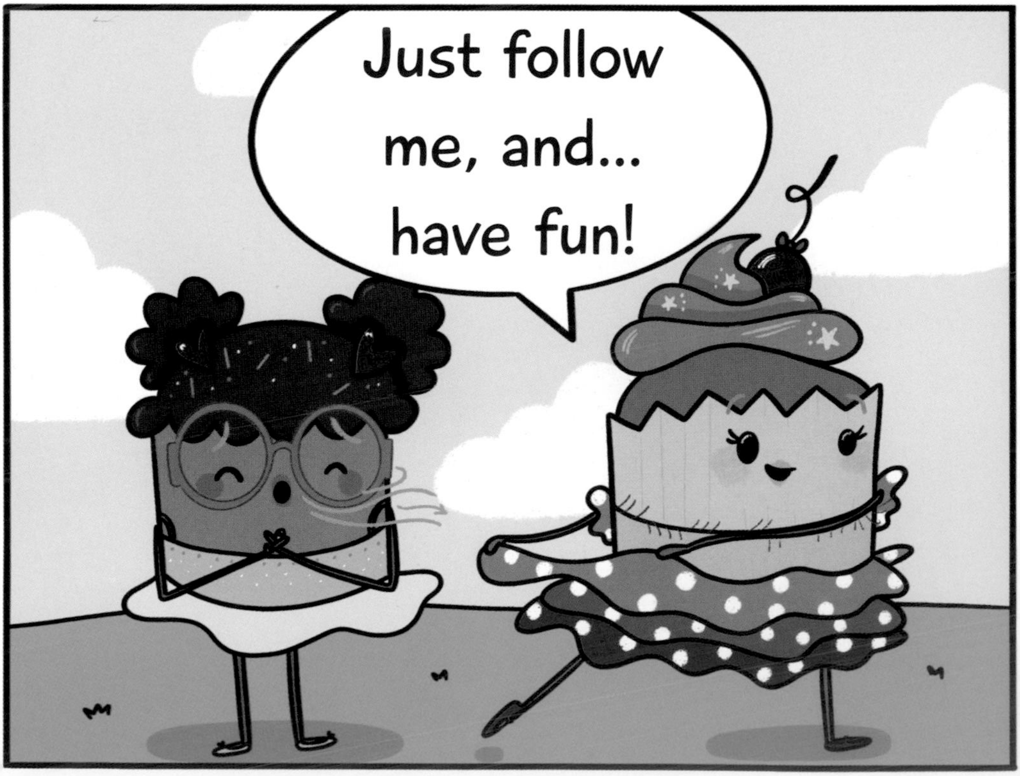
Just follow me, and... have fun!

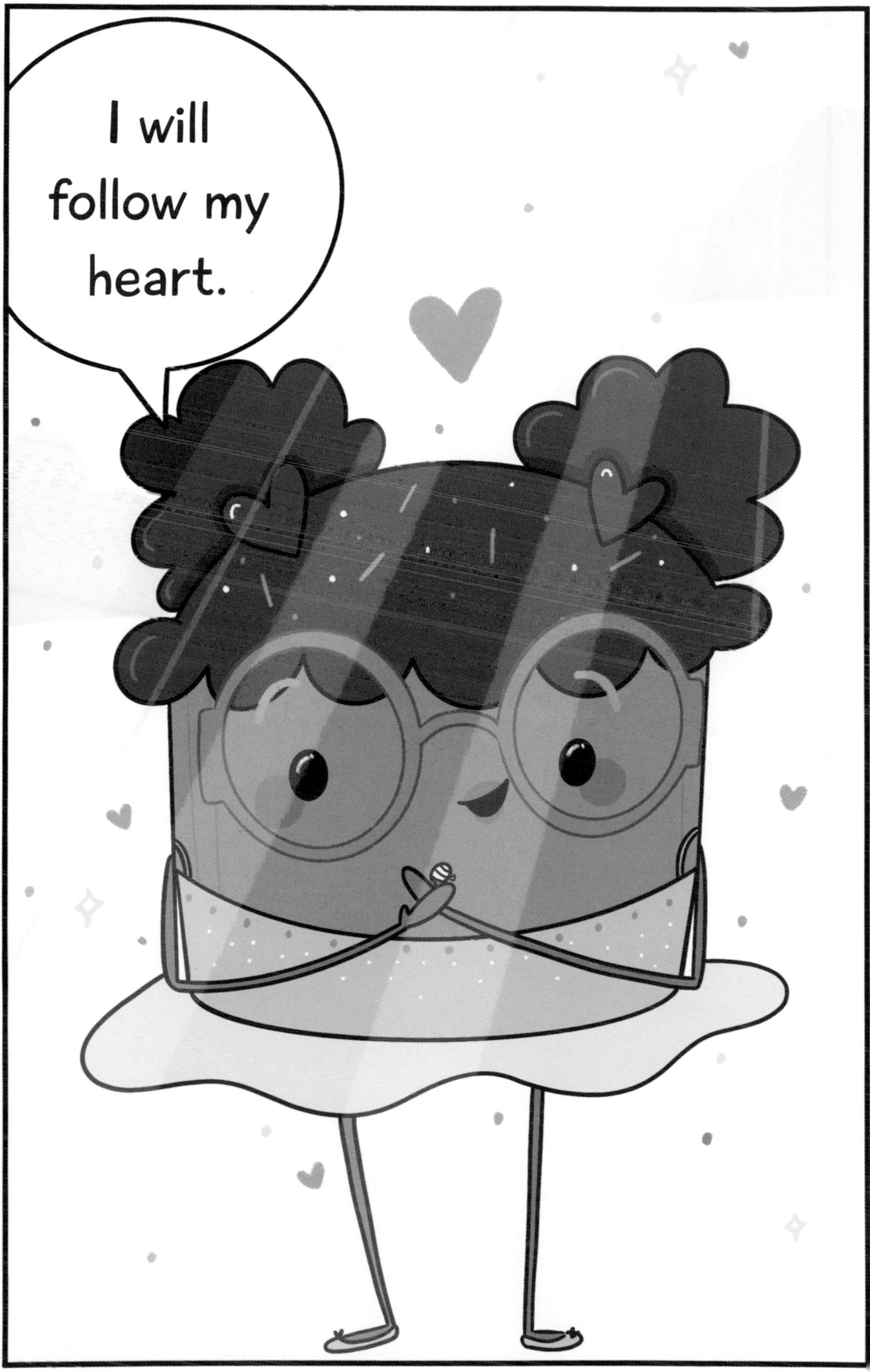
I will follow my heart.

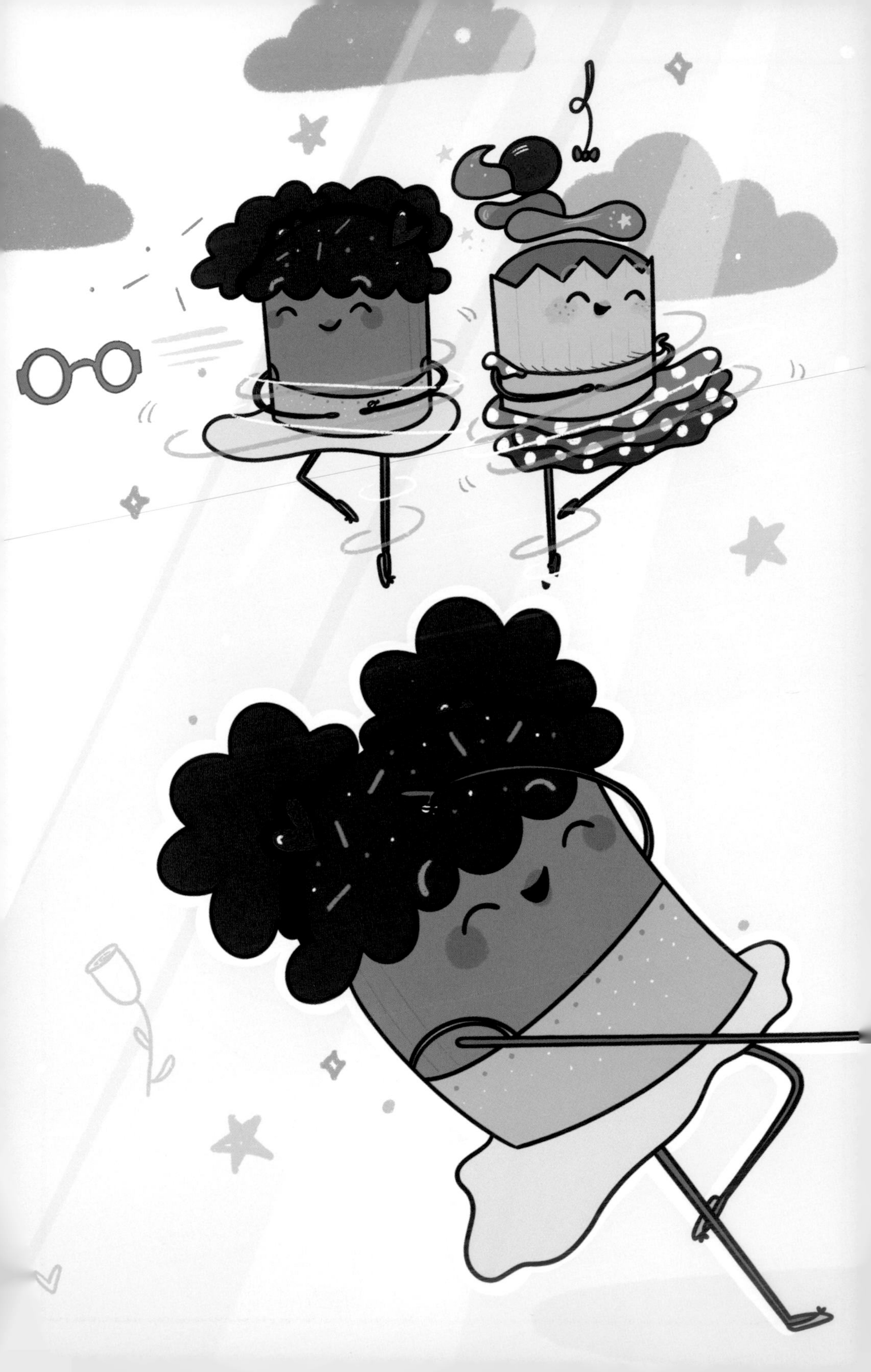

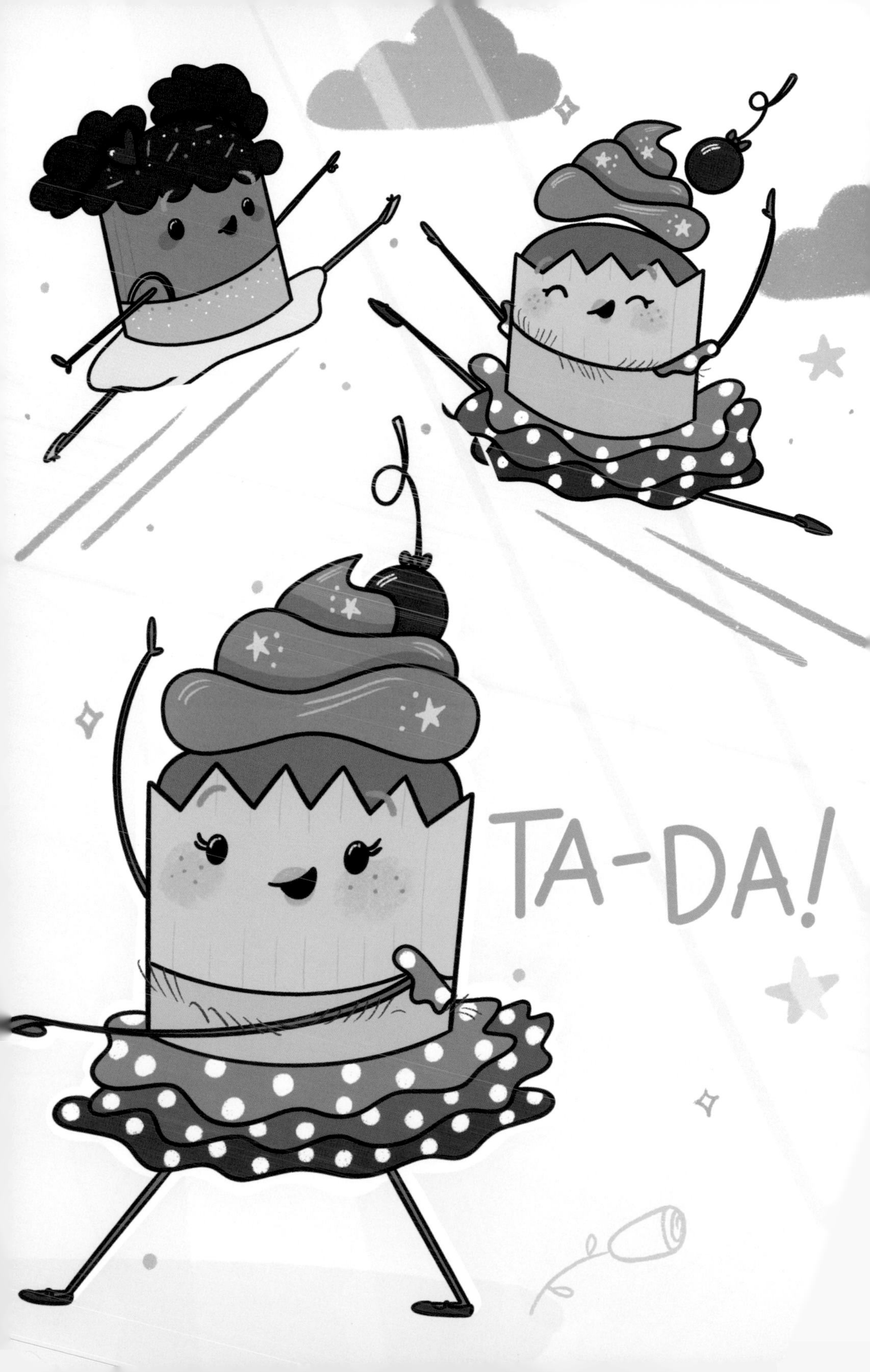
TA-DA!

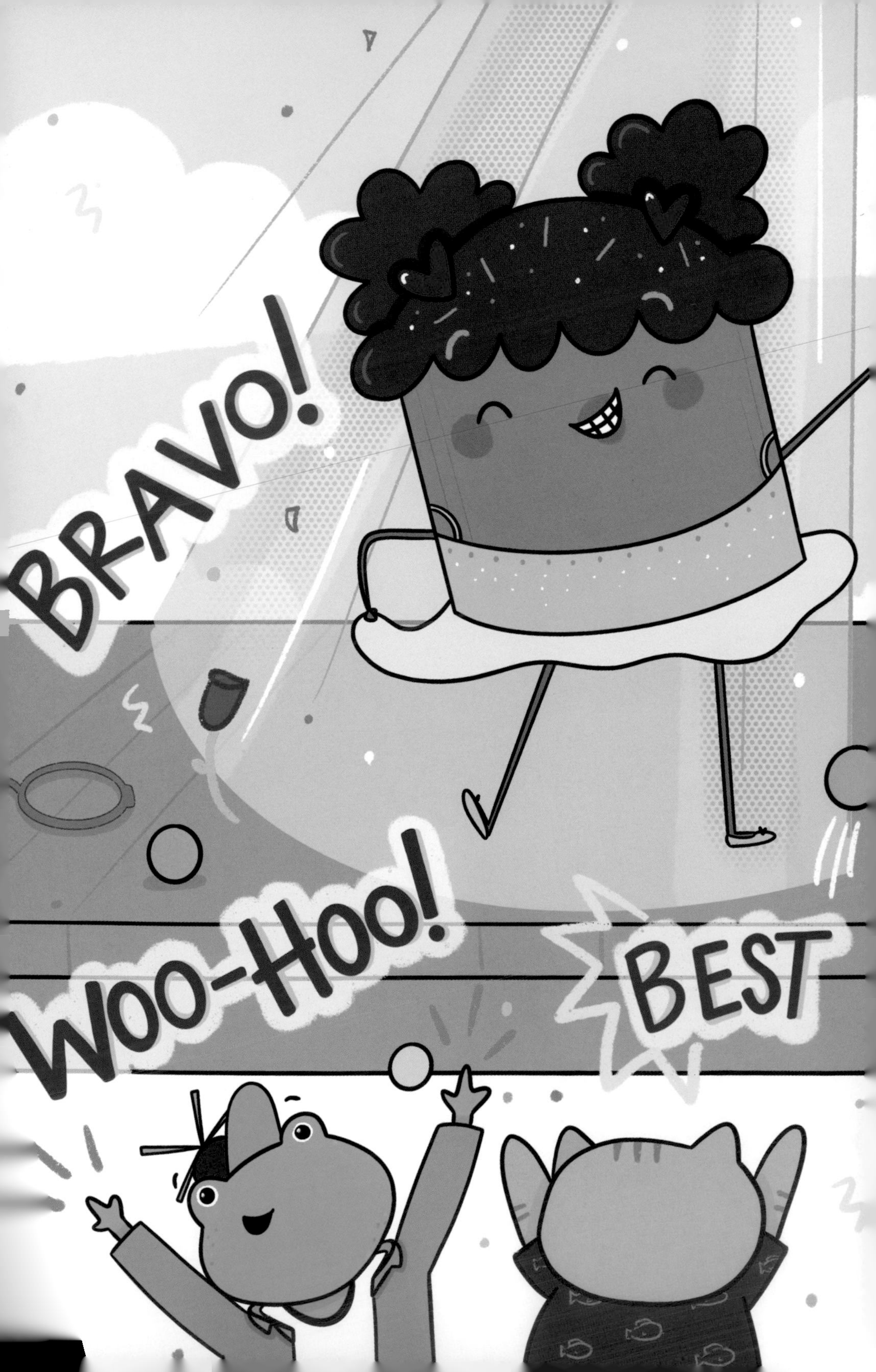
BRAVO!
WOO-HOO!
BEST

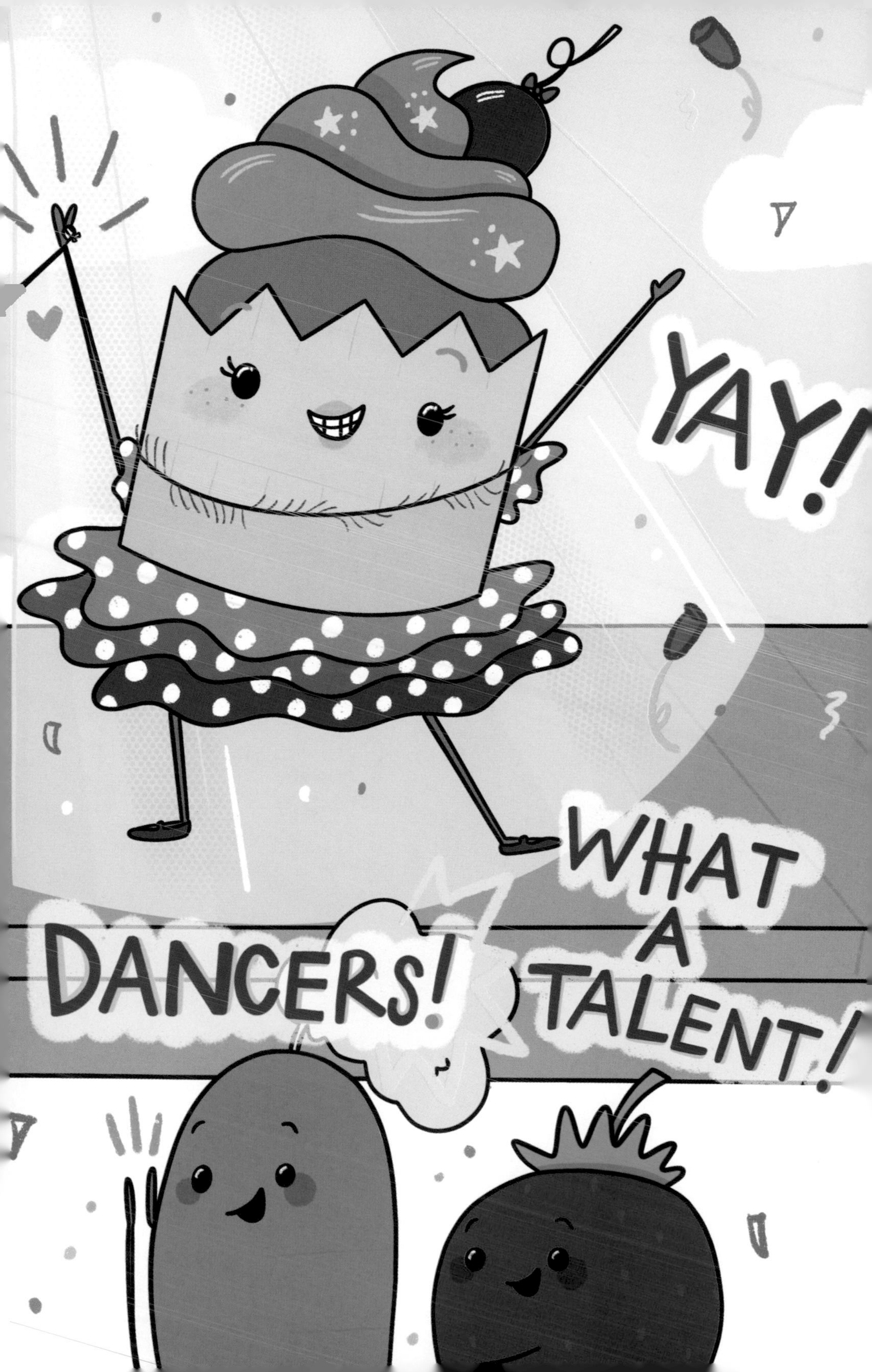
YAY!
WHAT A TALENT!
DANCERS!

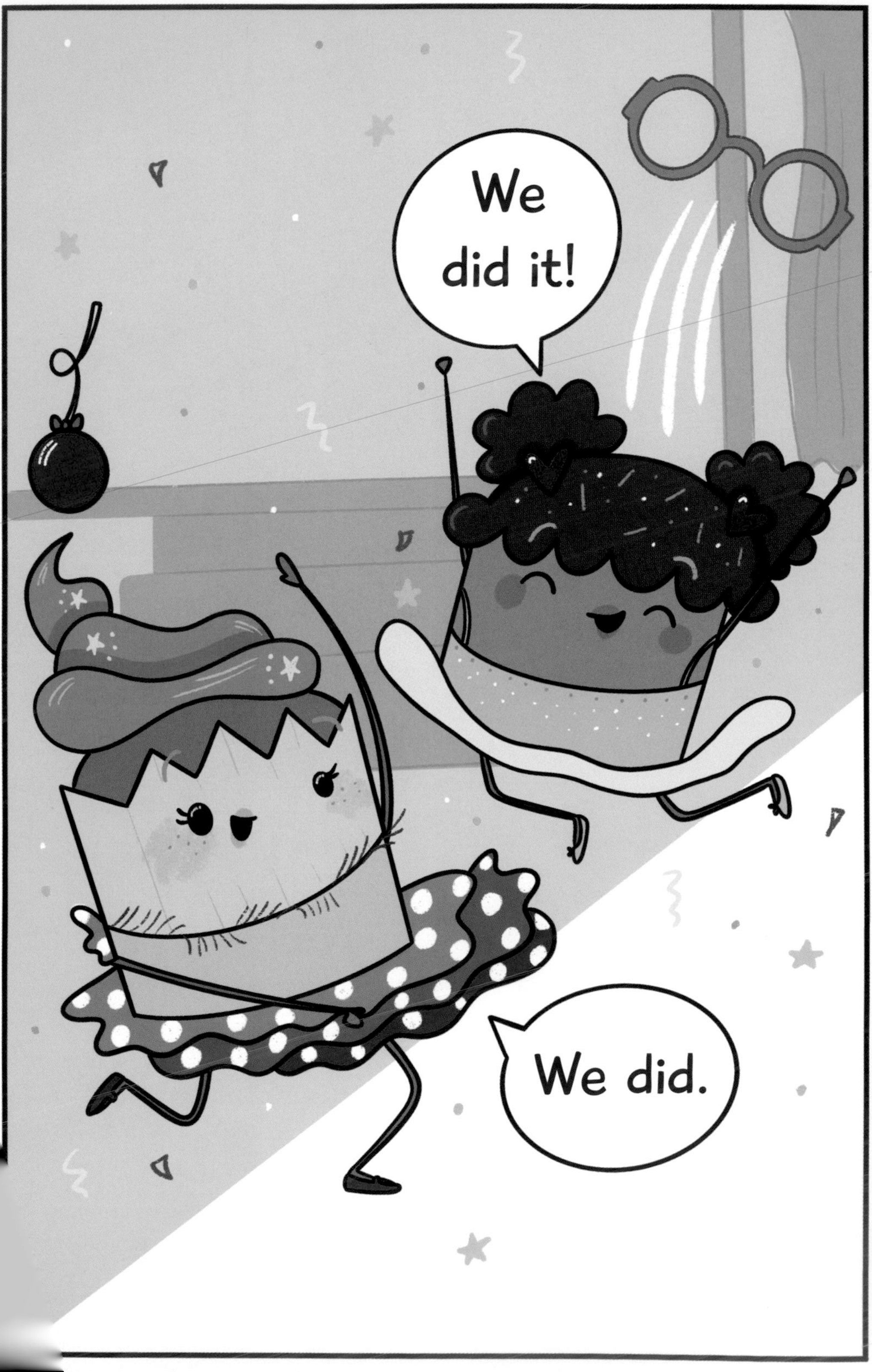
We did it!
We did.

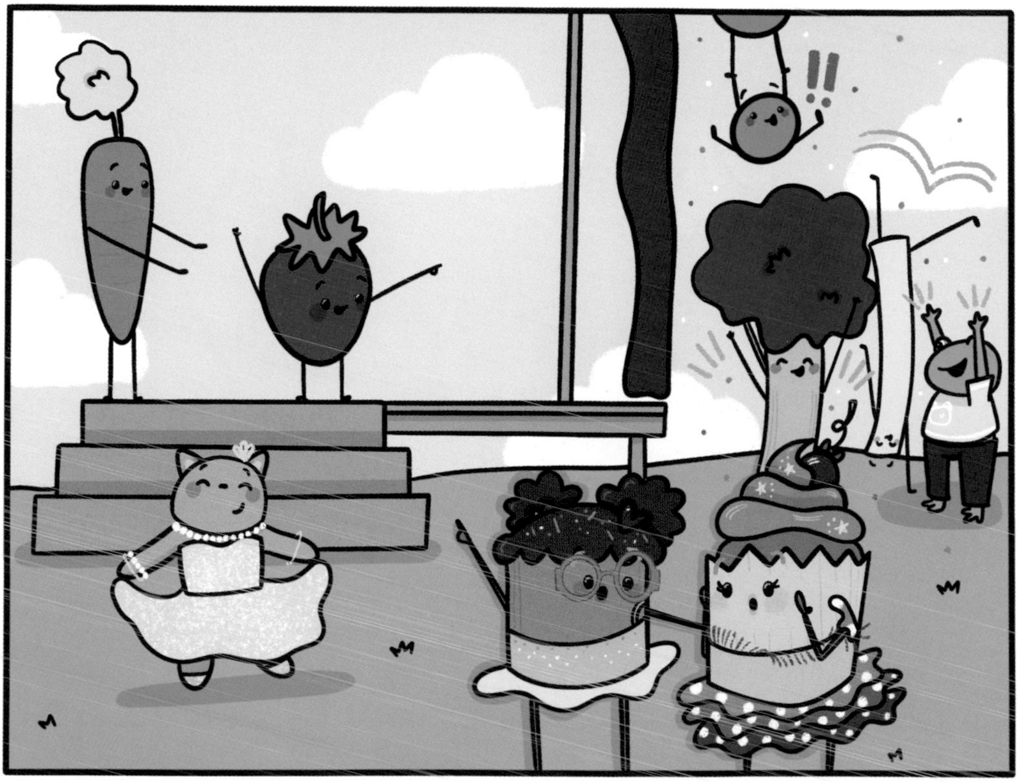

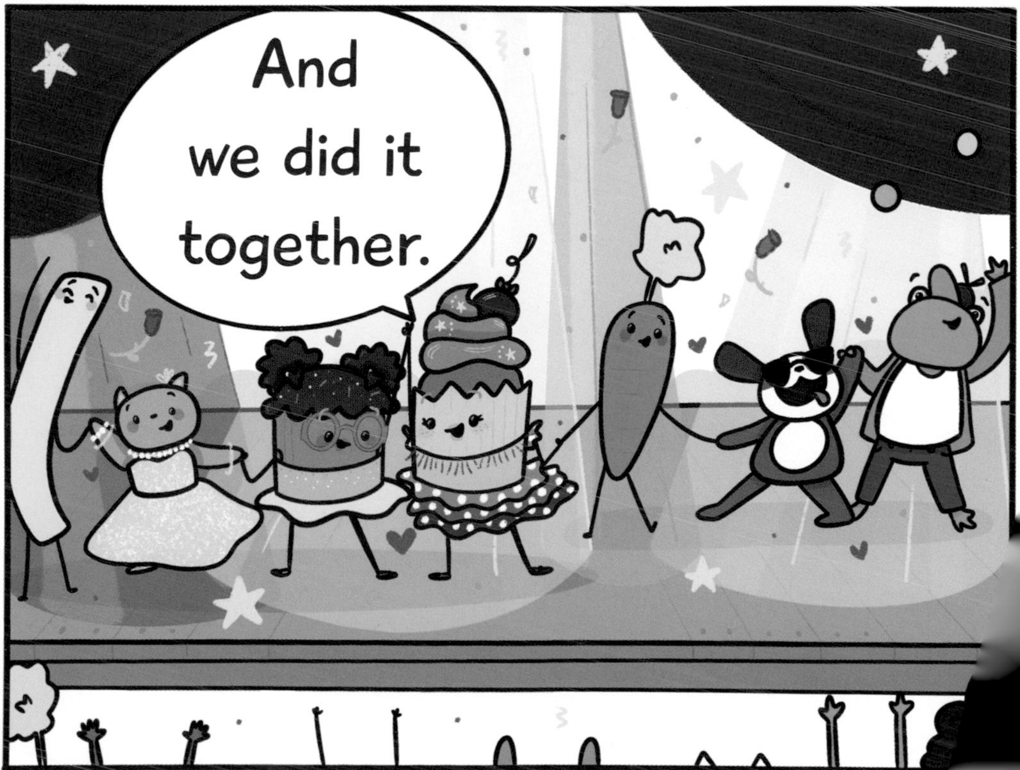
And we did it together.

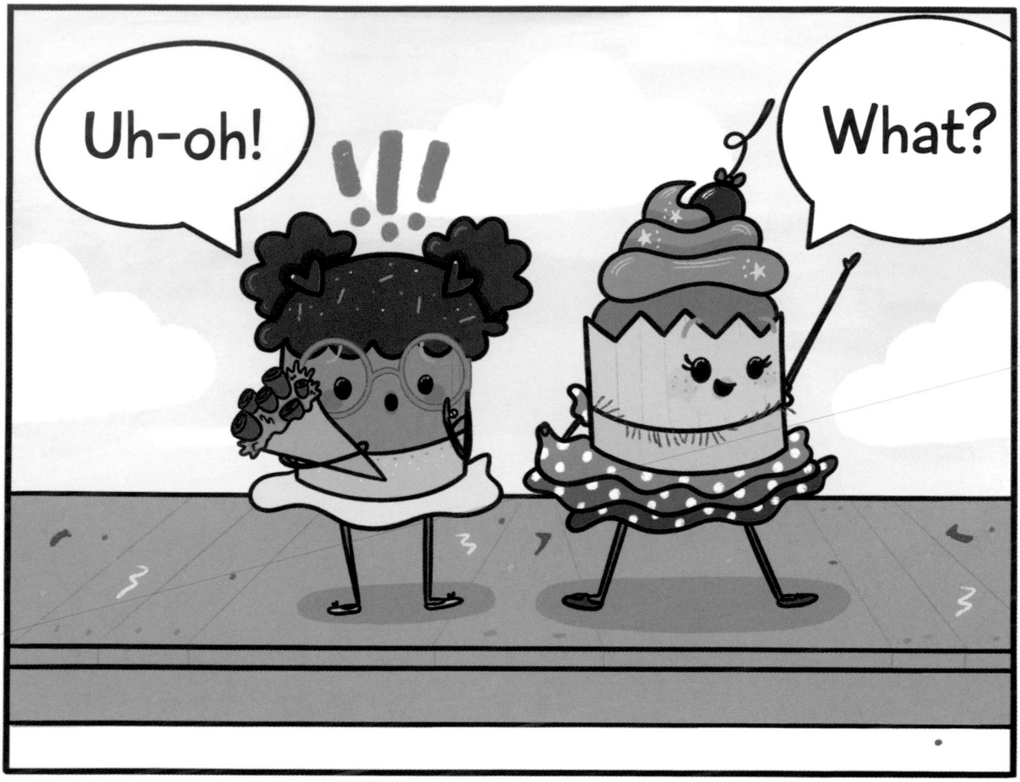
Uh-oh!
What?

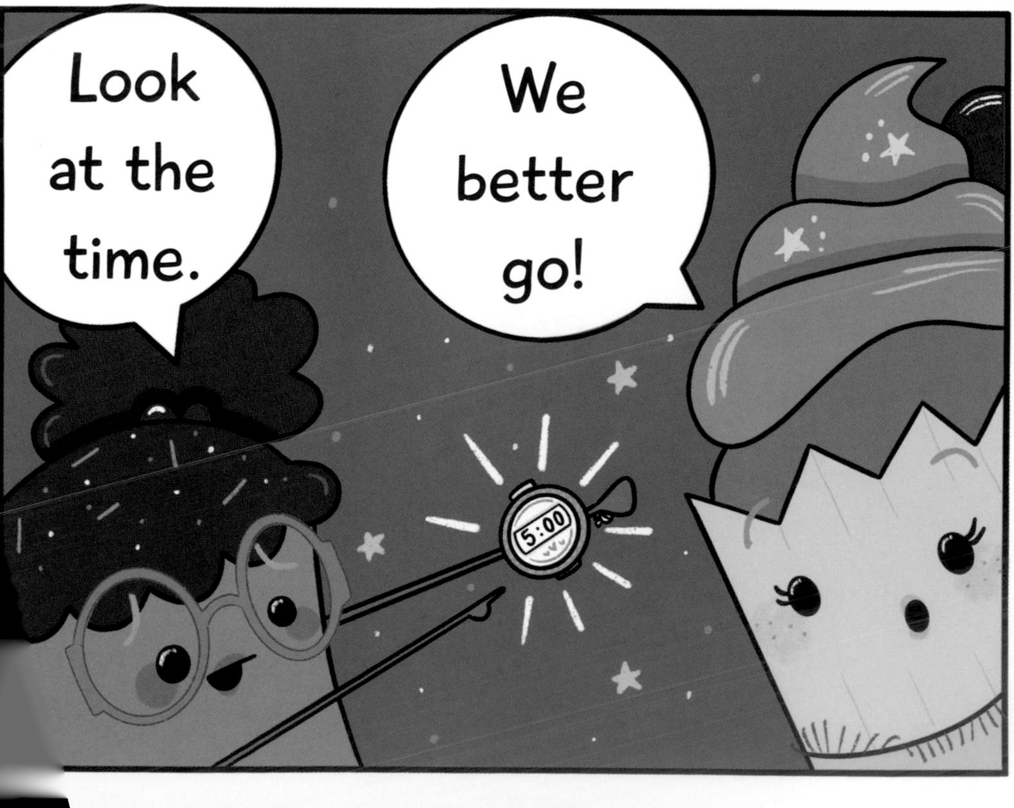
Look at the time.
We better go!
5:00

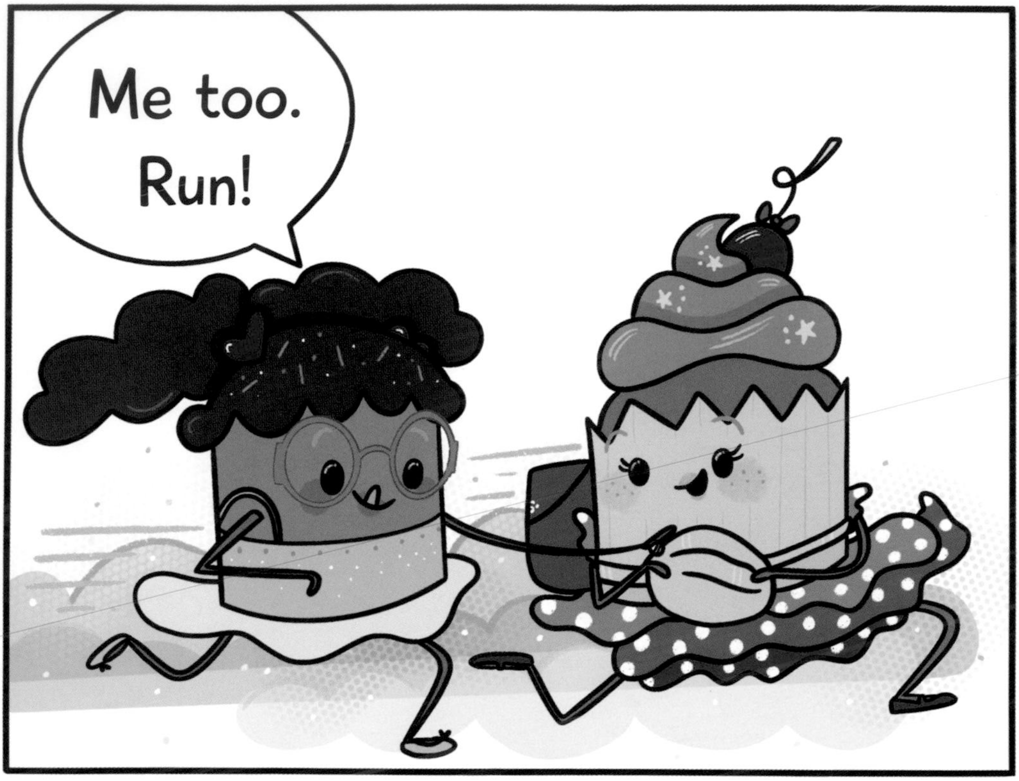
Me too. Run!

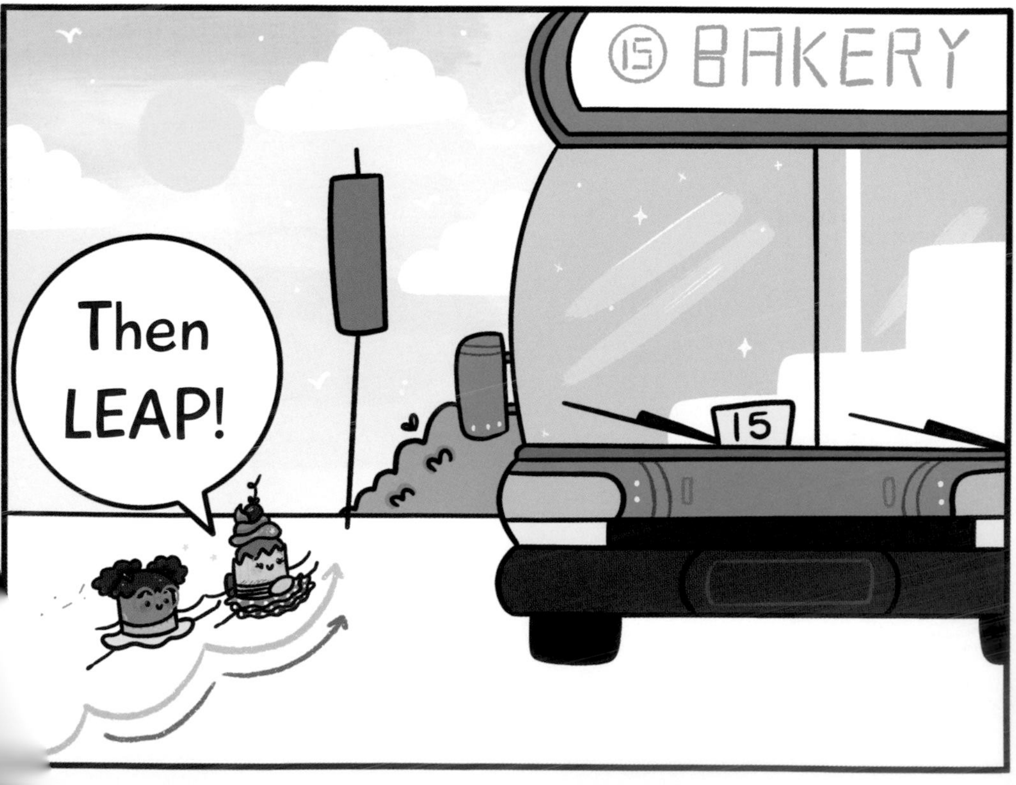
15 BAKERY
Then LEAP!
15

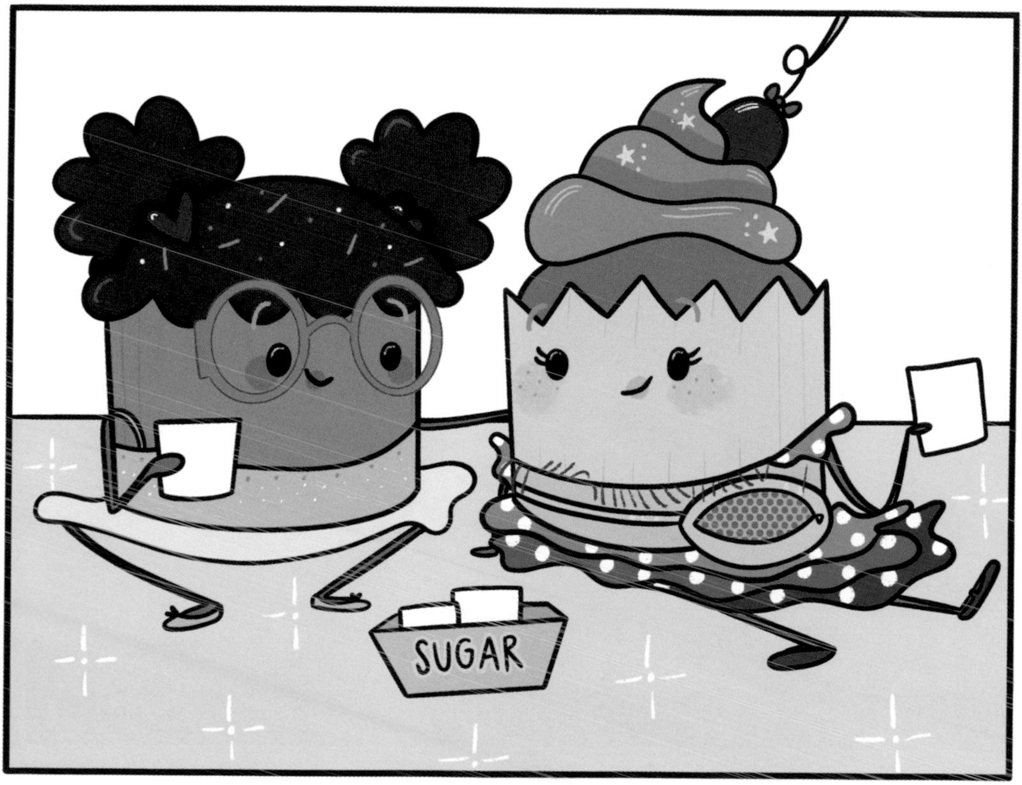
SUGAR

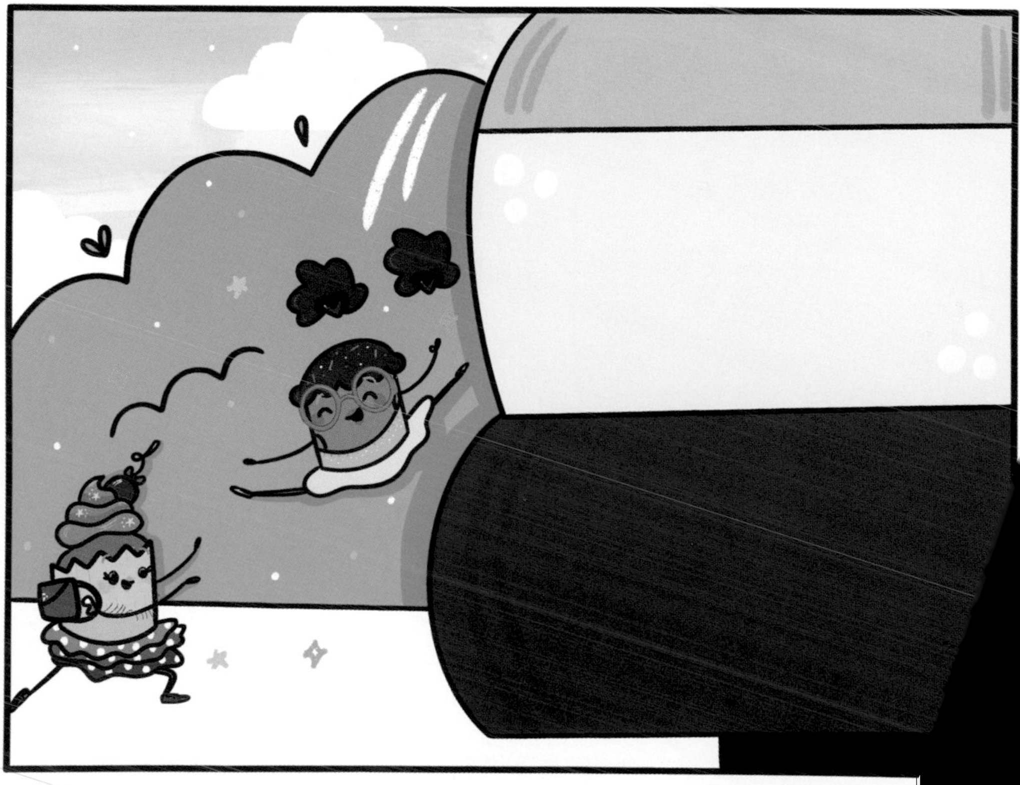

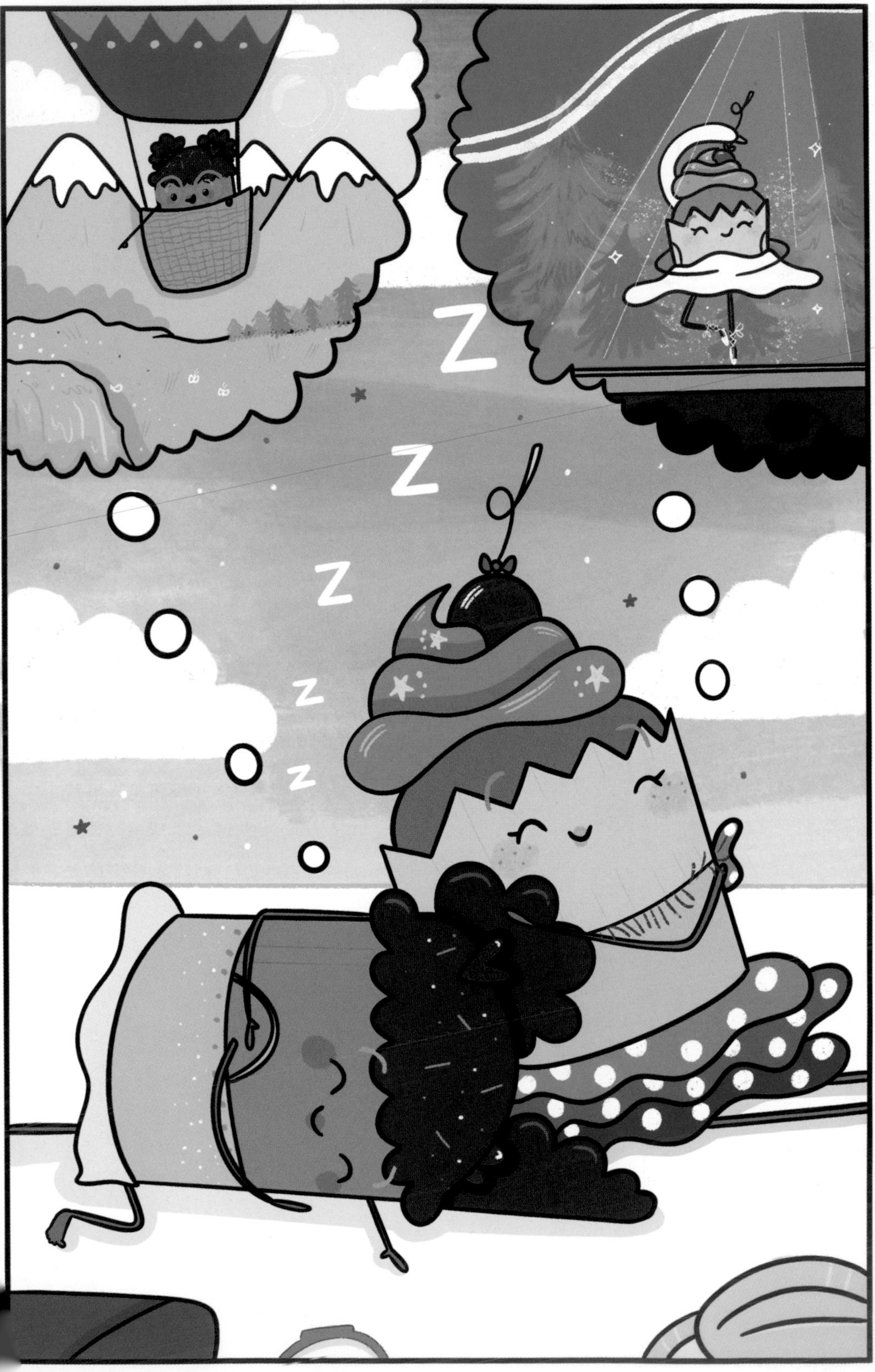
Z
Z
Z
Z
Z